She knew they had to be sensible!

"We'll both share the space blanket and our body heat, and you have my word I won't ravish you, okay?"

"And perhaps I should give you some assurances, too. That your basic forces are quite safe from me." She looked up then, her lips twitching. "But should I be overcome by the very worst, then I promise to give you fair warning, okay?" she challenged him.

"Sounds reasonable." He nodded with mock seriousness. "And I'd appreciate the fair warning. I'd hate to be caught unprepared," he added wickedly.

"I couldn't imagine it, Mr. Jerome."

"I do believe that was a rare compliment and I shall treasure it. Now, shall we go to bed, my dear?"

LYNSEY STEVENS, an Australian author, has a sense of humor that adds a lively quality to her writing. She has always enjoyed her work as a librarian—in a modern library providing children's activities, puppets, theater and other community services—but her first love is writing. Though her earlier attempts at writing historical and adventure novels were unsuccessful, and her first romance novel was rejected, Lynsey now has several published books to her credit. And she hints at the presence of a real, live Harlequin hero in her life.

Books by Lynsey Stevens

LYNSEY STEVENS

Touched by Desire

Harlequin Books

TORONTO • NEW YORK • LONDON
AMSTERDAM • PARIS • SYDNEY • HAMBURG
STOCKHOLM • ATHENS • TOKYO • MILAN
MADRID • WARSAW • BUDAPEST • AUCKLAND

ISBN 0-373-11643-8

TOUCHED BY DESIRE

CHAPTER ONE

THE small plane appeared to hang suspended, a bright white speck against the backdrop of a clear cobalt-blue sky over the dusty dry cattle country below.

Kris Quade sat in the pilot's seat listening subconsciously to the drone of the engine. Subconsciously. Consciously she was finely tuned to the tall man in the narrow seat far too close beside her. And in the almost claustrophobic confines of the Cessna 180 she could still feel his disapproval, his displeasure. In fact the air had been decidedly thick with it since their meeting less than an hour ago.

Arrogant, self-important, chauvinistic devil!

Yet he was by far the most attractive man Kris had ever seen. Certainly his photographs, the grainy black and whites that had been splashed over the newspapers in recent months, didn't do him justice at all. No wonder her cousin, Donna, had waxed so poetic about him. Kris could well imagine female heads turning for a second look as he passed by.

And wasn't it just typical that the manner didn't match the image? Nice packaging, but disenchanting inside.

She studied him surreptitiously out of the corner of her eye. Charisma personified. Not only did he have the looks, but even in her irritation and his ill-humour she was aware he possessed that rare sensual magnetism which, when he chose to use it to its fullest advantage, must be devastating. That she was not immune to that magnetism, considering what had transpired between them, completely astounded her, for it had been a long time since she had so much as looked at a man, let alone been so intrigued...

His hair was dark, reasonably long, but sat naturally back from his forehead, and where it touched his immaculate white collar at the back it had an uncharacteristic tendency to curl. Somehow those unrestrained fine dark strands of hair were his only saving grace, Kris reflected drily. There were flecks of grey over his temples, too, surprising as he was only thirty-four. Or so Donna had informed her.

His profile was totally masculine and could have been an ideal model for a sculptor. Forehead, nose, high cheekbones, square jaw—all so perfect. His chin was firm with just a hint of an attractive cleft. And a woman could drown in his eyes—an unusual shade of grey, she had realised. In the beginning she'd mistakenly thought they were dark, for they had been narrowed, glowing almost black as his anger rose.

Kris eyed her passenger appraisingly. Was he aware that this trip out to Amaroo, the Sorrel cattle station, had been but a smoke-screen for Donna's master plan? Kris would lay odds he didn't even suspect. Thank goodness!

'I've had the most incredible time,' Donna had stated on her return a week ago from one of her many jaunts to the city—trips on which Kris's pretty, vivacious cousin seemed to thrive.

As Rob, Donna's long-suffering husband, had remarked good-naturedly any number of times, heaven only knew what she found to do with herself in town, but it always cost him money.

Rob was at present overseas, so Donna's most recent stretch in the city had lasted for over a month. She'd arrived home with the usual parcels piled high, including gaily wrapped gifts for Rob, for their seven-year-old son, Josh, for her father, and for Kris.

Donna had chattered through her first meal at home that evening, relating all the social titbits, the snippets of gossip, making them all laugh. And it wasn't until dessert that she had rendered them speechless.

'And I've met just the man for Kris to marry.'

They all stopped eating, Kris almost choking on a mouthful of delicious sliced mango as Donna's words hung in the air.

'He's the most attractive, most gorgeous man you've ever seen, and he's pretty well heeled by all accounts. Not that that matters,' Donna added offhandedly.

'Of course not,' Ted Sorrel remarked drily, winking teasingly at the still stunned Kris.

'Oh, Daddy!' Donna tapped his weathered hand. 'He's something of a celebrity, I'll have you know.'

'Not a pop singer or anything like that, is he?' Her father frowned, suddenly serious.

'No. Nor an actor, nor anything unacceptable.' She raised her eyebrows with expressive exasperation. 'Actually, he's an accountant and has his own business. I suppose you'd call him a financial consultant or adviser. Very well known. And it's rumoured he's about to go into politics. The newspapers hint he'll be the Treasurer in no time and that he's headed for the top.' Donna paused for effect. 'They say it's a good bet he'll be the Prime Minister of Australia in the not too distant future.'

'Which party?' asked her father suspiciously.

'Who cares about that?' Donna shrugged. 'You always say they're all the same, Daddy. But can't you see Kris as the First Lady?' Donna appealed eagerly.

'You have to be joking, Donna,' Kris got out. 'Aren't you?'

Donna pursed her lips. 'Maybe I am, just a little. But you'd make a fantastic-looking couple. He's so dark and you're fair.' She sighed. 'Aren't you even a tiny bit curious about him, Kris?'

'Not really.' Kris took a sip of her wine. 'But I don't want to spoil your fun and you're going to tell me anyway so we might as well get it over with.'

'Todd Michael Jerome,' Donna announced with a verbal flourish, and her beaming face suggested there should have been a drum-rolling fanfare at the very least. 'Isn't that the most romantic name you've ever heard?'

'Todd Jerome.' Kris frowned. 'I think I did see something about him in the paper the other day.'

'Something about him! Ye gods!' Donna exclaimed in disbelief. 'The media has been full of him for weeks, months even. He grew up in Brisbane. His father was a carpenter and he comes from a large family, has half a dozen brothers and sisters, I think. He's thirty-four years old. And——' she'd obviously saved the best till last '—he's a bachelor.'

'A bachelor at thirty-four? Most men are married by then. What's wrong with him?' Ted Sorrel asked forthrightly.

'You weren't married until you were forty-two, Daddy,' Donna reminded him airily, and he scowled at her.

'That's different. I hadn't met your mother, God rest her soul.'

'And Todd hasn't met Kris,' Donna stated confidently.

'Kris isn't interested in marriage,' Kris's uncle said with conviction.

'Rubbish!' Donna exclaimed and then sighed loudly. 'It's been four years now since Kelvin died and Kris hasn't so much as looked at another man. Not even during the three years she worked in Townsville. It's way past time she remarried.'

'Now who's talking rubbish?' Ted Sorrel frowned. 'You're about as subtle as a hit over the head with a wet fish, Donna. Your cousin is quite happy as she is.'

'Oh, Dad. You just don't want to have to look for another housekeeper,' Donna began, and Kris diplomatically distracted them again.

'Your father's right, Donna. I'm not interested in remarrying. However, I'd hate for you to have gone to all the trouble of finding out about this Todd Jerome for nothing. The least I can do is listen to his attributes, if he has any—which I seriously doubt,' she added with a smile.

'Well,' Donna reflected, undaunted, 'I've only met him twice personally, the first time at an art gallery. It was so incredible. The crowd parted and there he was. I took one look at him and I knew he was the man for you, Kris. I went straight over and asked him to bring me a glass of champagne. Which of course he did.'

'Of course.' Kris suppressed a chuckle as young Josh screwed up his small nose and Ted Sorrel snorted loudly.

'Then we met again at a charity do just a week later. We had quite a chat. He's so intelligent. A financial whiz, you know. Anyway, to cut a long story short——'

'And we count our lucky stars for that,' put in her father and received a glare for his trouble.

'Mum, I've finished now. Can I go and watch television?' Josh got in smartly, with the ease of much practice when his mother had the conversation in full flow.

'Of course, love. Now, as I was saying,' Donna continued unabashed, 'I've asked Todd to give us some financial advice.'

Her father sat back in amazement. 'Do you mean to tell me he's going to try to teach you how to budget your monthly allowance? Then I say he's got his work cut out for him. But at least Rob may find himself solvent for once.'

'Don't be silly, Daddy. I mean Grandmother Warren's legacy.'

'Your half is tied up in trust for another two years, until you're thirty, and, in Kris's case, for four more years. Your grandmother showed a lot of foresight there. Although I'd have made it thirty-five,' he added sternly.

'Kris and I have to plan for it,' Donna told him earnestly. 'Todd says planning ahead is most important. I'll need to make the right investments when the money's in my full control. So will Kris.'

'There's no need for either of you to worry your pretty heads about things like that.' Ted patted her shoulder placatingly. 'We have our own advisers to handle it all.'

'Daddy!' Donna pouted. 'Kris and I don't intend to be empty-headed know-nothings. Todd says even if a woman's married she should be in control of her life, and that includes her financial security. Besides, it won't hurt to talk to him, will it?'

'I suppose not,' her father agreed grudgingly. 'And there's plenty of time, say next year——'

'How does next week sound?' Donna stated. 'Tuesday, in fact.'

Kris glanced across at her cousin in surprise. 'You're going back to the city next week?'

'No. Not exactly.' Donna grinned broadly. 'Todd's coming here.'

'He's coming all the way out to Amaroo?' Kris repeated in amazement. Only Donna could convince a man to drop everything and make the long journey into the outback for what amounted to a very premature consultation. 'Surely it would have been easier for you to discuss it with him in the city?'

'Ordinarily. But I wanted Daddy to meet Todd as well and I knew I'd never drag him away from his precious station.'

'Too right, love. That city scene's not for me,' Ted put in resolutely.

'Todd will be up north next week on business anyway, so——' Donna shrugged '—I arranged for him to fit us in.'

Kris suddenly turned cold. What was an amusing joke had now become cold fact. 'Us? Oh, no. How could you, Donna? I see now what you have in mind and I flatly refuse to have anything to do with it.'

'I don't know what you mean, Kris,' Donna said ingenuously. 'What's wrong with a little financial advice?'

'Financial advice, my foot!' Kris bit out. 'You're matchmaking. I thought you were joking, but bringing this stranger out here is carrying it a bit too far, isn't it?'

'He seemed quite keen to come——' Donna began, but Kris cut her off.

'I don't need anyone to find me a man. As a matter of fact I don't need a man, period. I'm quite happy as I am, thank you very much.'

'Kris, I understand,' Donna replied with quiet solicitude. 'I know how devastated you were when Kel was killed, but you have to start living again. Life goes on. Kel wouldn't have wanted you to isolate yourself. You know he wouldn't.'

'Donna, I don't——'

'I've just arranged for Todd Jerome to come out here for Dad to look him over. I mean, if I'm going to trust him to advise us on our investments I'd like Dad's opinion of him, seeing as Rob's away and can't do it.' Donna shrugged her shoulders innocently. 'There's just the added bonus that you can meet him as well.'

Kris held up her hand. 'I don't want to meet him.'

'Why not?'

'I just don't,' Kris said firmly. 'You can get all the financial advice you want, Donna, but I'm not looking over any prospective husband material, no matter how incredible his credentials are. He's probably the prime archetype of male superiority and I'm not into that.'

'Oh, Kris, don't be like that. Male superiority.' Donna laughed. 'That's silly.'

Kris gave her cousin a sceptical look.

'Rob says men have to use their brawn to get what they want while women must use their brains. And he says brains can beat brawn any time.'

'Rob's been with you too long, that's his trouble,' Kris remarked softly. 'And it always amazes me why he puts up with you.'

'Same here,' agreed Donna's father. 'If ever there was a long-suffering——'

'Enough,' Donna declared. 'I don't need you two ganging up on me. Rob loves me and I adore him and…oh, Kris, I just want you to be as happy as I am, as we are.'

Kris sighed. 'I know that, Donna, but I am happy. I don't need to be any happier at this time.' She sighed again. 'So you can get this Todd Jerome to give you all the financial advice you need and then he can return to the city. OK?'

Donna's eyes fell from Kris's before she nodded reluctantly.

'And I hope he's under no illusions about why he's coming out to Amaroo,' Kris stated emphatically. 'Right, Donna?'

'Oh, of course,' Donna replied airily. 'Did you think I would be that unsubtle?'

'I guess I'll have to give you the benefit of the doubt. So, does he know how far out we are?' Kris asked.

'Well, yes. Sort of,' Donna replied carefully, and Kris raised her dark eyebrows again.

She knew that evasive look. Donna had obviously glossed over the true facts, forgotten to tell the whole truth. The unfortunate Mr Jerome, who more than likely

had never been far from a city in his life, let alone left
a bitumen road for a gravel one, was probably all set to
take a taxi from Townsville.

'Oh, yes,' snorted Ted Sorrel. 'How's he getting out
here? Got his own private Lear jet, has he?'

'No. Of course not.' Donna frowned. 'I'm sure he'd
have told me if he had.' She shook her head. 'No, Kris
is bringing him out.'

'Me?' Kris's voice came out thinly. 'What on earth
are you on about, Donna?'

'Well, you're taking the Cessna into Townsville to pick
up those parts Daddy had on order. Daddy told me you
were flying them in on Tuesday when I rang before I
came home.'

As Kris gazed at her in amazement, Donna bit her lip.

'It was Tuesday, wasn't it? I mean, I didn't get the
wrong day, did I?' Donna appealed agitatedly. 'If I did
you'll have to go anyway, Kris. I told Todd I'd arrange
the transport. Have I mixed up the days?'

Kris shook her head. 'No, I am going in to Townsville
on Tuesday, but for heaven's sake, Donna, I don't par-
ticularly want to fly this—this stranger anywhere.'

'Why not?'

'Because now I know exactly why he's coming out here
you've put me in a pretty embarrassing position; you
must see that?'

'I can't see why. I told you I didn't tell him it was
especially to meet you. Honestly. And besides, he's absolutely gorgeous, Kris. I know you say you're not
interested in guys any more—you've told us often
enough—but even you'll have to agree once you see him
in the flesh that he's a real hunk.'

And so it had been arranged—no matter that Kris was
not looking forward to spending the flight with a man
she had never met, one she had had reservations about
right from the first. If all Donna said was true, and al-

lowing that her cousin was inclined to exaggerate, this Todd Jerome was still probably an egotistical pretty boy who thought every woman was going to fall at his feet.

Those ominous reservations she'd had about Todd Jerome had been spot-on, Kris reflected wryly as she slid another sideways glance at her passenger. They hadn't exactly hit it off right from the start.

Kris almost laughed out loud. That was putting it mildly. The air between them had seemed to explode with his anger and her indignation. It was a case of instant dislike.

Yet . . . was that strictly true? If she were honest she'd have to admit that in those first few seconds aversion wouldn't have been an accurate depiction of her feelings. She'd been momentarily nonplussed, numbed, and then an unfamiliar rush of blood had made her feel almost light-headed.

Of course she'd known what he looked like. Donna had described him at length and flashed those grainy newspaper clippings under her nose, but it hadn't quite prepared her for the Todd Jerome who had stood before her in flesh and blood dimensions.

Yes, he was attractive all right, and her spontaneous reactions to his physical magnetism had taken her completely by surprise. Kris had thought she was incapable of showing any interest in another man, especially one who had danger written all over every solid centimetre of him.

But feelings long dormant, sensations she'd thought had died forever with Kel, had stirred into instant attention, had set her nerve-endings quivering disturbingly. It was almost as though she were Sleeping Beauty, woken by Prince Charming's kiss.

The same heated glow rose to colour her cheeks.

Good grief! she admonished herself. She had to be kidding. The man beside her was not by any stretch of the imagination a Prince Charming. Prince Rude and Abrasive was more like it. Looks certainly weren't everything, especially in Todd Jerome's case. His opening statement back at the airport had instantly dealt her responses a killing blow and deepened her flush.

'Just wait for Todd at the airport,' Donna had said. She'd told him where to find the Amaroo plane and he'd be there at one o'clock.

So with over an hour to put in until the great man's arrival Kris had slipped an old pair of Kel's overalls over her jeans and cotton shirt, tucked her shoulder-length fair hair up under an old cap to keep it out of her eyes and any oil and grease, and begun her pre-flight inspection of the small aeroplane.

She had had her pilot's licence for six years now and she was a careful and competent pilot. She never took short cuts on her checks and the plane, although not a new model, was carefully and meticulously maintained.

She had just closed the cowling and was wiping her hands on an oily rag when a deep and obviously irritated voice behind her made her jump.

'I'm looking for Kris Quade?'

She turned around and there he was.

Todd Jerome. The epitome of a powerful male animal in his prime.

Kris's eyes began at his toes, encased in dark leather shoes—handmade if she wasn't mistaken. They moved upwards, over long legs, a narrow waist and a broad chest, resplendent in a charcoal-grey suit, an immaculate white shirt that would have done an advertisement for washing powder proud, and a dark, conservative tie.

Under his arm he'd tucked a leather briefcase and he carried a matching dark leather overnight bag.

And his whole stance, the expression on his ruggedly handsome face, mirrored his irritation, with perhaps a touch of boredom.

'This *is* the Amaroo Cessna, isn't it?' he asked imperiously and Kris could only nod, her mouth suddenly quite dry.

She swallowed convulsively. For once Donna hadn't been exaggerating. He was most definitely gorgeous.

Todd Jerome flicked back his shirt cuff and glanced exasperatedly at his wristwatch, giving Kris a flash of gold on a black leather band and fine dark hairs on a strong tanned wrist.

'Any idea how long the pilot will be?' he demanded, moving his gaze over the large hangar.

'No. I mean——' Kris swallowed again and tried to recover some composure, '—I'm here.'

Her fingers pulled fumblingly at the press studs down the front of the overalls and she began to shrug herself out of the sleeves.

'You!' he exclaimed shortly. 'You're just a kid.'

She was slipping the overalls downwards over her hips and as she stepped out of the baggy garment the rubber sole of her grey trainers caught in one leg and she had to hop inelegantly to regain her balance. He offered no assistance. Slightly flustered, she rolled up the overalls and pulled the cap from her head, her fair hair cascading in its natural waves to her shoulders.

'Hardly, Mr Jerome,' she said a little breathlessly. 'If you're ready, shall we go?' She indicated the door of the plane.

Todd Jerome closed his mouth, which had fallen slightly open in surprise.

'I beg your pardon?' The words came out after a pregnant pause during which, in turn, his grey eyes— for Kris could now see that they were a cold, steely grey— raked the length of her body from head to toe, then de-

liberately worked their way slowly back: over her jeans—
a favourite pair which were faded but comfortable—to
her loose pale blue and white checked cotton shirt, lingering suggestively on the mound of her firm breasts.

'If you're ready, we can go,' Kris repeated, fighting
the urge to fold her arms protectively over her chest as
her nipples suddenly hardened betrayingly against the
thin material.

'No way, lady!' He set down his bag and briefcase in
one decisive movement. 'Just tell me where I can find
Kris Quade. Where is he, anyway, and how long is he
likely to be held up?'

'He's not held up.' Kris's lips quirked and she sighed
shortly. 'Oh, for heaven's sake, I'm Kris Quade. Kristle
Quade, Donna Bradman's cousin.' She overcame the urge
to finish by asking him if he was incapable of comprehending anything other than a balance sheet.

His teeth clamped together, a muscle moving in his
tensed jaw. 'Donna told me...' he paused. 'Sorry—
Donna led me to believe her cousin, Kris, was a man
and a fully qualified pilot.'

'Might I suggest you simply took it for granted that
a pilot had to be a man?' Kris said evenly, and continued before he could comment, 'Well, Mr Jerome, I'm
female, and twenty-six years old, so I could scarcely be
called a kid. And I *am* a fully qualified pilot, make no
mistake about that.'

His cold eyes looked her over again. 'Yes, I concede
you're female, and at the risk of offending your apparent feminist leanings I have to say you don't look
twenty-six. But I don't have much time for women drivers
down here on the ground so I can't say I'm overjoyed
at the thought of being at the mercy of one in the air in
a small plane.'

Kris fumed, her even green eyes flashing. 'Aren't you
generalising, Mr Jerome? I'll grant you some women

drivers aren't very good, but then there are some male drivers who don't deserve a licence either. It's an individual thing, I would have thought.'

'Then we'll have to agree to differ.' He glared at her, his hands aggressively on his hips.

'We will, won't we?' Kris straightened and made herself move towards him and the plane. 'Shall we make tracks? I'd like to be home before dark. Or do you want to inspect my pilot's licence before you take the chance on getting off the ground with me?'

He raised one dark eyebrow provocatively as Kris realised what she'd said. She could have bitten her tongue at her choice of words and she strode past him as purposefully as she could, knowing colour washed her cheeks again.

Todd Jerome made no move to follow her, but he turned in her direction. Kris stopped by the small white aeroplane and regarded him levelly.

'You don't have to come out to Amaroo with me, you know. It's your choice, Mr Jerome. But I'm leaving in a few minutes and I'd appreciate it if you'd make up your mind. I can't see any point in wasting any more of my time bandying insults with you.' She swung open the door. 'If you're coming, pass me your bag.'

He muttered something under his breath—something Kris suspected was uncomplimentary—before picking up his briefcase and bag. With a wry twist of his lips he relinquished the overnight bag. 'Take note: I'm making no argument over who deposits that in the plane. I'd be the last to rail against the equality of women and I have a gut feeling you're a figure-head in the feminist movement, Ms Quade.'

'I'm sorry to disappoint you again, Mr Jerome, but I don't consider myself to be an active feminist.' Kris stowed his bag in the storage section. 'I just believe in the equality of everyone, male or female.' She climbed into her seat and waited for him to follow her. 'And by the way, to set the record straight, it's Mrs Quade.'

With an inexplicable spurt of triumph Kris reached for her seatbelt, only to come down to earth with a jolt as her shoulder and then her fingers came into contact with her passenger's as he folded his six-foot-plus frame into the narrow seat beside her. Sparks seemed to ricochet about the confines of the cabin, and by the time they'd sorted out the seatbelts Kris felt hot and just a little bothered.

'How long will the flight out to Amaroo take, Mrs Quade?' he asked as Kris shifted in her seat to get comfortable.

Had he emphasised the 'Mrs'? Kris wondered, and then dismissed it as a flash of paranoia in herself. 'Two and a half, maybe three hours. We should pick up a tail wind so perhaps a little less than that.' She reached out to switch on the ignition. 'All set?'

'What you mean, Mrs Quade, is do I want to change my mind and get out, don't you? The answer's no. Fate has placed me in what you've convincingly assured me are your capable hands. I'm afraid you're stuck with me for the next couple of hours, Biggles,' he finished mockingly as the engine roared into life.

And so here they were held captive in the small cockpit, flying north-west at six thousand feet in a clear blue sky. A few light cumulus clouds—fluffy white cotton balls—floated beneath them, casting flashes of shadows dancing over the dry ground.

Since they'd reached cruising height Todd Jerome had opened his briefcase on his lap and seemed engrossed in the sheaf of papers he'd taken from it.

Diligent *and* conscientious, apparently, Kris mused sardonically. Despite his silver-screen looks, the man was obviously a machine. Or perhaps that was simply the impression he liked to give. All work and no play.

Unbelievable. But he must socialise sometimes, for
hadn't Donna met him at an art gallery and then at one
of the many parties she attended?

Was he involved with anyone? The fact that Donna
had considered him as a prospective husband for Kris
surely meant he must be fancy-free. For all that her
cousin was given to organising other people's lives,
Donna wouldn't condone stealing attached men. Or Kris
didn't think so.

Still, moving in the circles he obviously did, Kris
couldn't see a man like Todd Jerome going short of
female company. He probably only had to nod his dark
head to have women queuing at his door, even allowing
for his abhorrent chauvinistic attitudes.

How could Donna have been so wrong? How could
she imagine Kris would even consider someone like Todd
Jerome after the quiet, reserved Kel?

Kris sighed and ran her eyes over the terrain below.
By now they should be in sight of the conspicuous
Southern Cross windmill that marked the Kangaroo
Number Two Well. She glanced at her wristwatch and
frowned slightly.

Ten minutes later there was still no sign of the windmill
and the hair on the back of her neck began to prickle.
Had they veered off course? She checked her instru-
ments. All appeared normal. She reached over and
tapped the compass. According to its reading they were
right on course. But they weren't. They couldn't be.

In earnest she searched the landscape below for a
familiar landmark, but could find none. Her mouth went
dry and she had to force her fingers clutching the controls to relax as her knuckles whitened. Something was
dreadfully amiss.

Kris reached for the handpiece of the radio and de-
pressed the button. 'This is Victor Hotel Sierra calling
Townsville Control. Do you read me, Townsville?'

There was absolute silence. Even the noise of the engine retreated into the background.

Kris repeated her message to no avail. For some reason the radio was dead, and no amount of dial twisting could raise even a bit of static.

'Is there a problem?' Todd Jerome asked, the sound of his voice breaking into her concentration, making her start.

'We seem to have lost radio contact with Townsville,' Kris replied vaguely and tapped the compass again, her ear tuned to the hum of the 225 hp Continental engine.

If she went down to a thousand feet she might be able to pick out their position, although she somehow doubted it, for she had a disturbing feeling that they were mysteriously way off course.

Kris throttled off and the plane began to descend. At about one thousand two hundred feet the engine coughed, faltered, and then resumed its hum. Kris ran her eyes over the gauges again. The fuel reading was fine. As she pulled the nose up to level at one thousand feet, slowing the speed down, the engine spluttered badly and suddenly stopped.

With cool precision Kris reached for the ignition, but it refused to fire. Perhaps the few revs she'd given the engine every thousand feet or so as they descended hadn't fully cleared the carburettor, or... Or what? she asked herself shortly.

The silence of the failed engine was almost deafening and Kris knew that every second was crucial. If she couldn't get the engine started now they would have no alternative but to go in and attempt a landing.

'We may have to land,' she told her passenger calmly, 'so you'd better stow your briefcase and check your seatbelt.'

She selected the fine pitch on the propeller so that she would get maximum power if the engine started, and pressed the ignition. But again nothing happened.

Kris's instincts took over. She trimmed the plane for gliding speed to get the best glide slope, lifting the nose to bring the speed back to seventy knots, still checking to see why the engine might have failed. Unconsciously holding her breath, she hit the starter again. Not a spark.

The altimeter showed six hundred feet now, and Kris knew they were committed to land. Cool and composed, she reached out and flipped the battery isolator switch to minimise the possibility of fire. Flashes of her forced-landing training and procedures clamoured in her mind as she looked below for a strip of flat ground suitable to put the plane down. There were a few scrubby trees on the left and a rocky outcrop on the right, but, although the space between them looked dangerously narrow from above, Kris knew she couldn't have asked for a better spot.

She watched the trees for the wind direction and prepared for a cross-wind approach. And she knew she only had one chance at it. There would be no practice runs.

The plane seemed to take ages to glide silently, eerily downwards. Kris held it off as long as she could and then the wheels hit the rocky ground. She braked hard, holding the controls back to keep the tail down.

And they would have made it but for the deep, narrow rut—a washout—that Kris had no way of avoiding. The wheels fell into the hole and, as if caught in slow motion, the plane flipped over, landing upside-down with a sickening crunch of metal on rock.

CHAPTER TWO

THE dust and grit that had accumulated on the floor of the plane cascaded over them, getting in Kris's eyes and mouth, but she was unaware of it.

'We have to get out.' She heard her own voice coming from somewhere far off and it sounded thin and high. There was no time to be hysterical, she told herself, and forced herself to take a deep, steadying breath.

'Are you all right?' she asked Todd Jerome as she heard a muffled oath beside her.

'Oh, fine, Biggles. Just fine.'

His reply was laced with his usual irony so she decided he must be unhurt. She pushed against her door with all her strength, but it wouldn't budge.

Beside her Todd Jerome let the buckle of his seatbelt go and he somehow managed to scramble right side up in the confined space. Then his arms came around Kris and she stiffened instinctively.

'Undo your seatbelt. I'll support you.'

Kris did as he bade her and fell in a flurry of arms and legs against the solidness of his chest. Breath hissed from his body, stirring the fair hair over her ear, and she struggled to find her feet.

'We have to get out of here. Can you get your door open?' she asked him quickly.

'Seems to be stuck.' He put his shoulder to it and held her back as she reached for the handle herself. 'Let me get my feet against it.'

He braced himself, and after a couple of heaves the door sprang open. Kris breathed a sigh of relief and Todd helped her through the opening before following her himself.

Standing out in the hot sun, a safe distance from the upturned plane, Kris felt her legs begin to shake, and she pulled herself together with no little effort. Those moments trapped in the cockpit had been horrific and yet had lasted less than a minute at the most. Their situation could have been so much worse.

'Blast that washout,' she muttered to herself. And for this to happen today, when she had on board Todd Jerome, who was probably the founder of some movement to ban women drivers from land, sea and air, was totally infuriating.

'I'm sorry about this,' she began with as much good grace as she could muster, but he cut her off with a short laugh.

'Undoubtedly, Biggles. But a mechanical malfunction is hardly your fault. You did a great job. It was a nice landing.'

Kris's eyes met his in surprise. 'Thank you,' she said in confusion, and he smiled. His grey eyes danced, crinkling at the corners, and deep creases furrowed his cheeks.

It was the first time Kris had seen him smile and her legs turned to water, and seemed to shake even more than they had a few minutes ago. Shock, she told herself. That was all it was. Delayed shock. But that smile was lethal, part of her acknowledged, and it crossed her mind that it would get him anything and anywhere he wanted.

'You're welcome.' He continued to smile. 'But if you were browned off with me for doubting your flying abilities you didn't have to stage such a dramatic example of your capabilities to prove your point, you know.'

'If you think,' Kris bit out, raising her hand to run it angrily through her hair, 'that . . .' She stopped in shock as she noticed the blood, dark against her fair skin. She examined her arm, but felt no pain and could see no wound.

Her eyes inspected the man beside her and she caught her breath, still more shock hitting her like a blow beneath her ribs. The leg of his trousers was torn above his left knee and a dark stain had spread downwards.

'You're hurt.' She moved towards him and he looked down at his leg.

'I think I caught it on something when we flipped over.'

Kris bent down to make a closer examination and her jaw tensed. The cut looked deep and ragged.

'The bleeding seems to have stopped,' he said as Kris stood up.

'I'll get the first-aid kit out of the plane. You'd better sit down, under those trees.' She pointed to a scrubby bush behind them. 'There's some shade there.'

His hand on her arm prevented her from moving. 'I'm not in danger of bleeding to death, so let's give it a few more minutes, Kris,' he suggested quietly. 'In case of fire.'

She nodded and they waited, watching for any sign of smoke or flame. Eventually Kris went to move, but his hand on her arm stayed her again.

'Let me check it out first,' he said firmly, and limped towards the aeroplane.

Kris wanted to follow him, but her knees were suddenly incredibly weak, refusing to carry her forward. Then he reappeared.

'No fire that I can see. Where's the first-aid kit?'

Kris told him and he reached into the cockpit and unclipped the white box from its position.

'At least we have well-stocked survival and first-aid kits, thanks to Uncle Ted. That's Donna's father. He owns the plane and he always insisted on that,' she drew herself together enough to remark as they walked away from the plane to a cluster of scrubby bushes and what was a patch of mottled shade of sorts.

'OK. Let's have a look at that cut.' She knelt down and attempted what she hoped was an encouraging smile.

'Let me guess, Biggles,' he said with now familiar mockery. 'Not only are you an ace pilot, but you moonlight as a qualified nurse or maybe a fully fledged doctor. Do you fly in, remove an appendix or two, and then fly out again?'

'No. None of the above. Just did a first-aid course.' Kris raised her eyebrows. 'And I am, I might add, the only aid you've got, first or otherwise. So let's clean this up.'

'I'm in your hands again, Biggles. Do I get a lump of wood to bite on? Or how about a stiff drink?'

Kris tried to ease the material away from his wound and she heard him catch his breath. His brows had drawn together and his dark hair fell forward over his forehead. For one split second she had to fight the urge to smooth it back.

'I think I'm going to have to cut away the leg of your trousers to clean it up properly.' Kris reached for the small pair of scissors in the first-aid kit and he grimaced, struggling to his feet.

Blood oozed from the gash, and Kris began to protest.

'And I think it will be easier and safer all round if I take the trousers off before you start wielding that dangerous-looking weapon.' He began to unbuckle his belt.

'There's no need to...' Kris began, dismayed at the prospect of watching this man undress.

His lips twisted, as much from pain as anything else, Kris suspected, and her eyes slid from the rasping sound of his zip being drawn downwards.

'Well, well. I don't believe it. Is that a maidenly blush?' he teased. 'I'm sure you've seen it all before, Mrs Quade.'

'Yes, but not yours,' Kris muttered, her mouth tightening as she turned defiantly back to him.

His dark brows rose. 'Then your horizons are about to be broadened,' he said outrageously and began peeling his trousers over his hips, wincing with the effort.

Without thinking, Kris moved towards him, helping him hold the material away from his cut until eventually they succeeded in removing his trousers completely.

He drew a sharp breath as he put his weight on his left leg, and now that Kris could see the extent of the damage the cut looked so much worse.

'You'd better sit down again,' she suggested and braced him as he lowered himself to the ground.

Kris tried valiantly to keep her gaze averted from his body, but her eyes betrayed her, sliding of their own accord over his long legs—legs that were well shaped and lightly covered in fine dark hair. They were also tanned and muscular, indicating that he didn't spend all of his time behind a sheaf of papers at a desk. She fought to keep her attention on his jagged cut, but she was powerless to prevent her eyes from roaming upwards...

For heaven's sake, what was wrong with her? She pulled herself up short. The man was bleeding to death while she sat watching, lusting after his undamaged parts. A soft sound, almost a giggle, escaped her, and she heard him draw a sharp breath.

'What's so funny, Florence Nightingale?' he asked, an edge to his voice, as he shifted on the dry, dusty ground.

Her eyes went to his. 'Nothing,' she got out, and tried not to smile.

'Female laughter is not something that usually follows when I drop my trousers,' he remarked levelly, and Kris put her hand to her mouth to hold back her chuckle.

She had the distinct feeling she wasn't far short of hysteria. 'I'm not laughing, exactly,' she began.

'No?' One dark brow rose in arrogant enquiry. 'Then perhaps I'm concussed. It sounded like a laugh to me.'

'It's just——' Kris paused '—delayed shock, I guess. From the crash,' she finished in a rush.

Her eyes returned to take in Todd Jerome again. No, women wouldn't laugh at this man, for Todd Jerome was the thread from which all feminine fantasies were woven.

'Well, what's the verdict on second inspection?' he asked softly, his voice deep and disturbing.

'I... What do you mean?' Kris mumbled, even more flustered.

'I think you know what I mean, Kris.' The sound of her name on his lips was almost her undoing and she sensed she had to dissipate whatever this tension was that was rising between them, drawing them into a dangerous cocoon.

'What do you think, Kris?' he repeated, and his magnetism was devastating.

Kris took a deep breath. 'I think, Mr Jerome, that we'd better fix up your cut. It seems to be bleeding again.' She reached for the first-aid kit, not meeting his eyes. 'It might hurt a bit, but I'll be as careful as I can.'

She grimaced with him as she began to clean the wound. Once she'd removed all the dried blood the cut didn't look nearly as bad, but Kris suspected it would need stitches when they reached a doctor.

'You were lucky, really,' she assured him. 'It could have been a lot worse.'

'A couple of inches higher and it might have been quite nasty,' he said drily, and Kris flushed at his meaning.

'Yes. Doubly lucky. My first-aid knowledge and jurisdiction stops mid-thigh.' She tried for a lightness she certainly didn't feel.

He gave a muted laugh, a low, husky tone, probably tempered by the pain he must be feeling, yet the sound ran through Kris like liquid silk, soft and so smoothly sensual.

She glanced up at him. He had paled and a fine film of perspiration dampened his brow. 'I won't be much longer. If you can just hold this dressing in place I'll bandage it up.'

Her fingers suddenly became all thumbs and she had to take a firm control of herself so that she could complete the operation. She was thankful when it was finished and she could move back from him.

'Do you have another pair of trousers in your bag?' she asked him, folding the torn pair over her arm. 'Long ones will prevent sunburn.'

He nodded. 'There's a pair of sunglasses in my bag, too.'

He made no demur when Kris returned to the plane and heaved his overnight bag out of the jumbled mess behind the seats. She allowed herself time to take a few deep, steadying breaths. She had to pull herself together, and quickly.

Perfect as his body was, she reproached herself, this was scarcely the time or the place to start thinking about . . . well, thinking lecherous thoughts.

She felt a surge of heat rise through her body, setting her senses tingling, colouring her cheeks.

It had been four years since she had experienced that particular quickening in the pit of her stomach, the yearning to . . . She reined in her train of thought.

Yet for one completely insane moment she wished . . . Kris turned purposefully back towards the patch of shade where Todd Jerome sat, refusing to allow herself to so much as acknowledge any such thoughts.

'There's a pair of white cotton surf trousers on top,' Todd Jerome said as she put his bag down and began to unzip the first compartment.

She found them and passed them to him, helping him as he climbed into them. 'At least it's not the middle of summer so it won't be as hot as it could have been. But you'll be glad of the long trousers tonight when it gets pretty cool.'

'Tonight?' Todd repeated. 'So you don't anticipate our rescue is imminent?'

Kris considered prevaricating, but decided he deserved to know the truth. 'Not today, anyway,' she said quietly. 'It will be dark soon so they won't be able to continue the search.'

'Any idea where we are?'

'No,' Kris replied reluctantly. 'There could be a slight problem for the search aircraft because the compass in the Cessna was malfunctioning. I have to admit it was my fault entirely for not noticing sooner that we had veered off course. I've flown the route from Townsville to Amaroo so often I should have picked it up miles back. I wasn't taking much notice of the landscape below and I should have been.'

Instead of being so busy watching and thinking about you, she wanted to add, but didn't.

'How far off course do you think we are?' he asked evenly and Kris shrugged.

'I really don't know. But once they've searched our flight path they'll fan out until they find us.'

'We could be in for a long wait, then?'

'I'm afraid so. But we have plenty of water and survival rations in the plane,' she reassured him quickly.

'"A Jug of Wine, a Loaf of Bread—and Thou Beside me singing in the Wilderness"?' He grinned at her and that now familiar quickening in the pit of her stomach took hold of her again.

'No bread or wine, just biscuits and water.' Kris smiled faintly, and his eyes seemed to be locked on the curve of her lips.

And she suddenly recalled Donna's conviction that this was just the man for Kris. No! No way. Not Todd Jerome. This man spelled danger in bright red letters a mile high.

'It will give us time to get to know each other,' he said at last when Kris thought the tension between them would explode into hot, bright sparks about them.

She stiffened as all of her senses clamoured her peril. He was far too charismatic, too attractive. They were too isolated. And she was far too vulnerable.

'There's not much to know, I'm afraid, Mr Jerome. I'm just an ordinary, rather boring person.'

'That I don't and won't believe.'

'It's true, I'm afraid. Now——' she rezipped his bag and stood up, '—as I only have this short-sleeved shirt I'm going to change into my overalls to protect my arms from the sun and then I'll brew us a cup of tea. Or coffee if you prefer.' She went to walk away from him, but his hand on her arm halted her.

'Kris.'

Her eyes met his and then fell quickly to where his strong fingers rested on her bare skin. Slowly he released her. But not slowly enough, she thought, and had to school her features as she took herself exasperatedly to task. Yet her skin felt aflame where he'd touched her.

'I think you'd better call me Todd, don't you? It seems a little ludicrous to stand on ceremony out here.'

Kris managed to incline her head before continuing on her way.

Night fell quickly and Kris shivered as she flicked on the torch lantern. 'We'll probably wake at dawn so we may as well conserve the batteries in the lantern as much as possible and have an early night.'

'Is there any chance we can get the radio working?' Todd Jerome asked as he shifted the position of his damaged leg.

'I don't know. I'll have a look at it first thing in the morning, but unfortunately I'm not a radio mechanic.'

'You surprise me, Biggles,' he said drily. 'I was beginning to think there was no end to your many talents.'

'Will you please stop calling me Biggles?' Kris bit out. 'I have no earthly idea what connotations the name has, so whatever dig you're having at my expense is completely wasted on me.'

'No digs, at least not the way you mean.' He grinned, his white teeth flashing in the dim glow of the artificial light. 'I take it you didn't read any Biggles books when you were a kid?'

Kris shook her head.

'It used to be on the radio, too, but before my time,' he explained. 'Dad and my older brothers were radio fanatics and it was one of their favourite shows. *The Air Adventures of Biggles*. As I grew up the books were put in my hands as sort of compulsory reading, and they weren't half bad as I remember. Biggles was an ace pilot so...' He shrugged. 'Biggles. It was a compliment.'

'I'm sure,' Kris said sceptically.

'Really. You are a crack pilot, Kris,' he assured her softly. 'Not many pilots, male or female, could have brought the plane in like that.'

'You forget, Mr Jerome——'

'Todd,' he put in.

'You forget, I crashed it,' Kris repeated wearily.

'Through no fault of your own. We're both in one piece, aren't we?'

Kris nodded. 'Well, almost.'

'I rest my case. And this——' he indicated his leg '—is just a scratch.' He picked up his coffee and took a sip as he watched her over the rim of the plastic mug.

Kris shifted uneasily. This conversation, his intent gaze, was getting too personal. 'You mentioned older brothers. Do you come from a large family?' she asked, settling on the first thing that came into her head.

'Five brothers and one sister. I'm the youngest.'

'Wow! It must have been, well...' Kris sought an unprovocative adjective.

He grinned. 'Busy. Noisy. Stormy. But it was great. How about you? Any siblings?'

'Unfortunately not. I always wanted to be part of a large family, but my father died when I was just a toddler, and my mother when I was twelve. Uncle Ted, who's my mother's brother, took me in and gave me a home, so I was pretty lucky there. He was wonderful to me and treated me like a second daughter.'

And as an only child I yearned for lots of babies, Kris wanted to add. But Kel and I decided to wait. And we waited too long.

'So you're Donna's only cousin?' he asked, and Kris nodded.

'Yes, there's just the two of us. Why?'

'No reason. I just didn't connect Donna's cousin Kris the pilot with Donna's female cousin who lived on Amaroo.'

'Oh.' Kris gave him a sideways glance. How much had Donna told him? She'd said she hadn't been unsubtle. That could mean anything. Perhaps, Kris decided, she should try to ascertain exactly what Donna had divulged.

'I believe you were going to give Donna some advice on her investments?' Kris began warily.

'That's right. We met in Brisbane and she asked for my help. She told me her husband has no head for business as he's more involved in the practical running of Amaroo and his adjacent family station, Claymore Downs.'

Kris smiled. 'That's quite true. Rob's a man of the land. And now that Uncle Ted's getting on in years Rob's taken over managing the two stations together.'

Rob had such pride in his job, Kris reflected silently. He looked upon himself as caretaker of the land and stock, until he could hand it over to his own son, Josh.

A frown drew her brows together.

'Kris? What is it?' Todd sat forward.

'I was just thinking about Josh. And how worried he'll be.'

'Josh?'

'Donna's young son,' Kris explained. 'He's seven years old. He'll... they'll all be so worried about me.'

'They must know you're a good pilot so they'll be thinking positively, won't they?' he said levelly.

'Yes, but the waiting.' Her voice faded slightly and she made herself straighten her backbone. 'What about you? Your family? They'll be concerned too.'

'I'm sure they will, but I can't see them dwelling on the worst.'

'And what about...?' Kris paused, 'I mean, are you involved with anyone?'

At any other time or place Kris knew she couldn't have asked him that. Yet here, stranded in the outback, the question seemed quite acceptable.

'No, not at the moment.'

He didn't elaborate, and some imp inside Kris forced her to probe teasingly.

'And you're not going to be a kiss and tell, apparently.'

'Never that,' he replied in an amused tone. 'I guess I've had my share of broken hearts, but none that I haven't recovered from in due course.'

'And I'll bet you've done your share of heart-breaking,' Kris commented, and his head came up, his lips twisting.

'Now what could you mean by that, Mrs Quade?'

'Just that you... that there must have been a lot of... you know what I mean,' she finished in a rush.

'No. You tell me.'

Kris held his gaze, knowing she'd ensnared herself in this embarrassing topic of conversation. 'You must know that you aren't the most unattractive man around,' she retorted drily. 'I merely meant there must have been a lot of women who thought they'd fallen for you.' My happily married cousin thought you were the catch of the century, she added to herself.

'Only *thought* they'd fallen for me?'

'Do you usually find it necessary to fish for compliments?'

'No. Only with you,' he said softly, and Kris heard the warning bells clanging inside.

'I was simply making conversation before, serious conversation.' She frowned at him.

'When?'

'When I asked if you . . .' She sighed exasperatedly. 'Look, all I meant was is there someone special who will be worrying about you?'

'My mother. The rest of my family. My father died some years ago. But no wife or special girlfriend, no.'

Silence grew between them, a tense, uneasy hush that had been absent before, and Kris shifted uncomfortably and shivered slightly.

'Are you cold?' he asked and she shook her head.

'Not really. But it will get colder as the night wears on.' She stood up. 'There's a light rug and the space blanket in the survival kit here so we'll be warm enough.'

She picked up the space blanket and held it out to him. 'Wrap yourself in this with the shiny side in.'

'Ah, one of the marvels of modern technology.' He pushed himself to his feet and took the sheet from her. 'And what about you?'

'I've got this rug.'

His face was all hard angles in the shadowy light. 'Very noble, Biggles. I'm all right while you freeze to death with a pious look on your face.'

Kris drew a sharp breath. 'I assure you I won't freeze to death, and what do you mean by "a pious look on my face"?'

'Pious,' he repeated. 'Sanctimonious. Saintly. And, above all, faithful to the end.'

'Faithful,' Kris reiterated between her teeth. Somehow he'd managed to confer a multitude of meanings on that simple word, and none of them gave the impression that it was at all commendable.

'Faithful. Loyal. Impeccable reputation. As a matter of fact you sound like the perfect little wife straight out of some syrupy TV sitcom.'

Kris felt herself stiffen and she lifted her chin. 'I do happen to uphold the sanctity of marriage, Mr Jerome, if that's what that snide remark means, and that includes being faithful, loyal and devoted. I realise it may sound old hat in the circles you move in, where anything may go, but I'm afraid I do believe in it and I'm damn sure I'm not going to apologise for it to you.'

'Nice sentiments, Biggles. But even the best of convictions have a habit of going out of the window when other more basic forces take over.'

'In *your* experience,' Kris threw back at him.

He inclined his head mockingly.

'Then I feel very sorry for you, Mr Jerome. You must have been mixing with the wrong type of women.' She held his gaze levelly and a peculiar excitement began to race through her veins. 'Or were they the right type of women to accommodate your——' she paused for effect '—"more basic forces", hmm?'

He stood silently regarding her for long, tense moments and then he gave a low erotic laugh. 'For a pious little paragon you can hit uncharacteristically way below the belt, can't you?'

'I felt it was deserved,' Kris told him, mortified that her better self and her own 'basic forces' seemed to be waging a battle within her, and even more ashamed at the realisation of which instinct she wanted to win out in the end.

Why did this particular man have the power to do that to her, to reach deep inside her and bring that previously concealed, totally uncharted and definitely unacceptable facet of her personality to the fore, to mock and disturb her?

'You're probably right, Kris.' The tone of his voice had changed. Gone was the sarcastic bite, and the even huskiness that had replaced it was so much more threatening, more unnerving.

Without being conscious of it Kris felt her own sense of truculence, of confrontation leave her and she began to relax a little, leaving only that purely physical tension to taunt her. And part of her realised, cautioned that at this moment he was at his most dangerous.

'I'm sorry,' he said softly. 'I didn't mean to tease you. I just don't want you to spend a cold and miserable night at my expense. Look, we're in a critical situation and we have to be adult about it. Our survival could depend on it. So let's be sensible. We'll both share the space blanket and our body heat and you have my word I won't ravish you. OK?'

Kris swallowed. Put so reasonably, what could she say? And he was right—it was the most sensible thing to do. But...

'All right,' she got out at last.

'Unless you ask me to ravish you, that is.' He gave that throaty chuckle that reduced Kris's legs to watery weakness. 'Sorry again, Kris. My little joke. You tend to bring out the comedian in me.'

'Really? Then just don't give up your day job!' Kris kept her face expressionless as she spread out the old rug as a groundsheet of sorts. 'And perhaps I should give you some assurances, too. That your basic forces are quite safe from me.' She looked up then, her lips twitching. 'But should I be overcome by the very worst then I promise to give you fair warning. OK?' she challenged him.

'Sounds reasonable.' He nodded with mock seriousness. 'And I'd appreciate the fair warning. I'd hate to be caught unprepared,' he added wickedly.

Kris laughed softly. 'I couldn't imagine it, Mr Jerome.'

'Todd,' he repeated easily. 'And I do believe that was a rare compliment and I shall treasure it. Now, shall we go to bed, my dear?'

CHAPTER THREE

'WHICH side of the bed do you prefer?' he asked her informally.

'I... I really don't mind.' Kris couldn't prevent the slight stammer in her voice. It had been so long—four years—since she had shared a bed with Kel.

'Neither do I.' He lowered himself on to the rug beside her, grimacing as he shifted his leg into a more comfortable position.

'Is your leg aching?' she asked him, intrepidly trying to relax her tensed muscles as his arm brushed hers.

'Not at the moment. The pain-killer you gave me is doing its job.'

'Well, goodnight, then,' Kris said stiltedly.

'Goodnight, Kris. Sweet dreams. And you can rest easy. As much as I hate to admit it, and at the risk of ruining my reputation, this leg will pretty well rule out ravishment for tonight.'

'Every cloud has a silver lining,' she said softly and he chuckled.

'Ouch! Need you be so wounding, Biggles?'

Kris knew instinctively that he was smiling and her pulse raced erratically. At this rate she'd be unable to sleep a wink.

'And incidentally.' His deep voice flowed over her, only firing her physical awareness of him. 'As we appear destined to be marooned out here I'm glad you were Cousin Kristle and not the expected Christopher Quade.'

With that he settled down and soon he was breathing evenly, obviously asleep.

Surprisingly Kris slept too, emotional and physical exhaustion taking its toll, and as dawn broke she woke revived, although somewhat stiff, unaccustomed to the hard ground.

They spent the day trying not to continually scan the hot sky for the sight of a search aircraft. Using stones and debris from the crash site they set out a large 'SOS' sign on the open ground so that it would be easily visible from the air.

With Todd's help Kris emptied a couple of small crates in the cargo of their crashed plane and set them up in the shade of the scrubby trees, with the space sheet now rigged as a canopy over them to afford them as much shade as possible. They sat on top of the upturned crates as they knew the temperature wasn't as intense three feet off the ground as it was at ground level.

But as night fell Kris had to bite back a sudden rising panic that clutched at her throat and made her feel agitatedly breathless. She inhaled slowly and deeply, knowing she had to keep calm.

In the glow of the lantern she turned to find the glitter of Todd's eyes upon her. Unconsciously she straightened her back and managed to give him a wry smile.

'I guess we're stuck with each other for another night.' Her voice sounded almost normal.

'It seems we are.'

Was there an amused quirk to those firm masculine lips? Kris rather suspected there was. It was no laughing matter, she wanted to snap at him, but arguing wouldn't help their situation. She swallowed her ill humour. 'I'm sorry about the radio,' she began and he shrugged.

'Can't be helped. I'll have another look at it tomorrow. I guess we'll just have to stay put until someone flies by.'

'Yes.' Kris's heart sank. A slim chance normally, but they were missing and there would be an organised search. Surely tomorrow...? They couldn't be so far off course that they would never be found. Could they?

No! She mustn't even think such thoughts. She was being ridiculous. Of course they would be found. It was only a matter of time.

'Was this your first emergency landing?' Todd broke into Kris's tortured thoughts.

'Yes. In all the times I've flown between Amaroo and Townsville or Cairns, or even down to Brisbane, I've never really considered finding myself in this situation. Oh, we went through the motions in training, but it wasn't exactly the same thing,' she added with feeling.

'You passed with flying colours,' he said softly, and Kris was compelled to meet his gaze again.

Her heartbeats began to race once more and it had nothing to do with memories of those all too swift seconds preceding their crash-landing. There was no denying that the reasons for her breathless inner turmoil were purely sybaritic now and Todd Jerome was solely responsible.

He had the most seductive voice of any man she had ever heard. When he lowered his tone that way it was like sipping a mellow tawny port. He was simply breathtaking, weaving a cocoon about her, enmeshing her, holding her hostage.

She felt like a knight deprived of his armour, vulnerable to Todd Jerome's devastating magnetism. And all this from half a dozen feet away. What would her reaction be should he reach across, touch her...? It would be so easy to be lured beneath his spell, to fall in love with him.

In love! Kris hastily pulled herself together, glad of the semi-darkness that shielded the rush of deep colour to her cheeks. Was she mad? Had the heat of the outback sent her a little insane, or 'troppo', as the locals laughingly described it? Falling in love, indeed! She had to be deranged. She'd known the man for less than forty-eight hours and she was thinking about...spinning ludicrous fantasies like a naïve schoolgirl.

She really had to nip this folly in the bud, find some strength, some will-power to keep him at arm's length. And she had to remember her forceful words to Donna. She didn't need a man at all.

'Did you always have a burning desire to fly a plane?'

Kris blinked as she forced herself to concentrate on his words, rather than the low, lethal timbre of his voice.

'To fly?' she repeated, trying to instruct her sluggish mind to compute his question. 'No, not really. I don't remember thinking about it. It just happened, seemed sensible, I guess.' She swallowed, almost under control now. 'You see, Uncle Ted needed someone besides himself to pilot the Amaroo plane and Kel, my husband, wasn't keen on flying. Kel always suffered quite badly from motion sickness so I suppose I was the obvious stand-in.

'As a matter of fact, Kel was my first passenger.' She smiled nostalgically. 'He even brought along a bottle of lemonade and we drank a toast at six thousand feet. He was nauseous for a couple of days afterwards.'

'He sounds like quite a guy,' Todd said flatly and Kris eyed him suspiciously, suspecting he was being sarcastic.

'Yes. I've yet to meet anyone as nice, as pleasant and as uncomplicated as Kel,' she finished with a tilt to her chin.

'Quite an act to follow,' he said so softly that Kris couldn't be sure she'd heard the words and a tight silence held them for long, emotive moments.

'Where did you meet your husband?' Todd asked, his tone back to normal, effectively defusing the heavy disquiet that screamed around them.

At school,' Kris told him, and laughed as Todd raised one fine dark brow. 'Honestly. We met when I was twelve.'

'A childhood romance,' he remarked with a touch of scorn, and Kris's smile faltered.

'Unimaginative, I know, but I suppose it was just that,' she said defensively, and he continued as though she hadn't spoken.

'So, let me guess. You and Kel were a couple all through school. Everyone expected you to marry and you didn't disappoint them.'

'You make it sound—well, boring. But I can't see anything wrong with two people who love each other getting married. It was what we both wanted.'

Todd held up his hand. 'I didn't mean to ridicule, Kris.' His mouth twisted derisively. 'Put it down to my cynicism.'

Kris smiled reluctantly, not noticing the intent way Todd Jerome's eyes moved over her face to dwell on the tender curve of her lips. 'I suppose it was pretty clichéd,' she acknowledged. 'We were married when I was eighteen.' She shrugged. 'End of story.'

Well, not quite, she finished inside. The end came in a dusty outback gully when Kel's horse had stumbled and fallen.

'And what did you and Kel do for excitement for those idealistic pre-nuptial years?' The sarcasm was back in Todd's deep voice and Kris regarded him levelly.

'We didn't need the kind of excitement I think you mean,' she stated composedly.

He raised one dark brow mockingly. 'No? And I suppose you had every right to wear virginal white as you came down the aisle.' He paused. 'And later that night?' he added meaningfully.

Kris flushed. 'Not that it's any of your business, but Kel and I both wanted to wait for our wedding night. Was that so wrong?' she challenged.

His eyes glittered in the light of the lantern as he watched her. 'For you, I guess not,' he said quietly.

Tension grew again and once again it was Todd who broke it.

'And what was it like?'

'What was what like?' Kris's throat was raspy and dry.

'Your wedding night. Was it worth all those years of waiting?'

Kris blushed, staring at him in disbelief. 'Don't you think that's being a trifle rude? I mean, you can't go around asking questions like that. It's...it's... Well, it's——'

'Improper? Impertinent? Impolite?'

Kris felt sure that he was getting a great deal of enjoyment out of disconcerting her.

'I admit I don't usually,' he assured her without any obvious signs of contrition. 'But this is different.'

'I fail to see how,' Kris put in reprovingly.

'Out here. Alone. Stranded.' He shrugged.

'I really can't see that our position makes any difference at all. Out here or somewhere more accessible, I still consider you're being offensive.' Kris regarded him directly.

'But this situation does rather strip away the thin veneer of civilisation, don't you think?'

Kris shifted uneasily at his words. What did he mean? And what did she really know about this man, this stranger?

'All right.' He spoke then, as Kris's throat began to dry at the scene her imagination threw up before her. 'I apologise if you feel I've been rude,' he continued quite graciously and paused. 'But did you enjoy it?'

'Enjoy what?' Kris was having trouble keeping up with the discussion.

'Your wedding night,' he reiterated patiently.

'Of course I enjoyed it,' Kris burst out exasperatedly before she could prevent herself. 'What else did you expect me to say? It was nice.'

'"Nice"! A little bland, wouldn't you say, Biggles? Didn't the earth move?'

'Look, I think we should end this topic of conversation right now.'

How could he sit there and ask such intimate questions without caring if he embarrassed her or not? He was superficial and shallow, tactless and downright rude.

'And,' Kris continued with as much scornful dignity as she could muster, considering the devilish smile that had lifted the corners of his mouth, 'I have no intention of discussing my sex life with you or anyone, Mr Jerome. Besides...' She paused and glanced down at her hands clasped together on her lap.

Now was the time to tell him about Kel, inform him that she had been a widow for four years. Wasn't it?

'Besides?' he prompted.

But something held Kris's words back. At the moment she had the presence of Kel to hide behind, to protect her to some degree, as a last bastion against the magnetism of the man sitting far too close to her in the circle of light. As a widow she would be open season. But with her husband in the background, surely he wouldn't...?

Unless Donna had already told him she was a widow. No. He'd have said something, surely? She gazed at him from beneath her lashes, wishing she knew what he was thinking.

'Let's just change the subject,' she said tiredly.

'Pity. And just when we were getting to the good bits. I was about to ask you if the inimitable Kel was the faithful type?' He raised those mocking dark brows challengingly and Kris's rose again.

'Of course.' Kris managed to keep her voice even. She had no intention of mixing it with him again tonight. She had to make him aware that he wasn't going to provoke her again as he was obviously trying to do.

'Of course,' he repeated drily. 'And what about you?' he continued. 'Never had the slightest urge to stray?'

'No.' Kris's mouth dried.

And she hadn't. Not during her marriage and not once in the four years since Kel's death.

Not until she met Todd Jerome. The words sprang into her mind, taking her unawares, and she grew hot all over.

He was watching her in the dim light, his eyes bright gleams in the shadowy angles of his face.

'There's no point in getting married if you still intend to play the field, is there?' she asked him with just a touch of irritation, irritation directed more towards herself than him.

Todd shrugged easily. 'Those sentiments are commendable and fine until the honeymoon's over. How did you know you or Kel wouldn't meet someone you were attracted to and found you couldn't resist?'

'That's hypothetical and hardly worth thinking about. If you're quite happy within your marriage I see no need to look for that sort of thing,' Kris assured him.

'But it can seek out and find you, Kris,' he said in that low liquid tone, and she shifted on her crate to disguise the shiver that passed over her.

'I don't think so,' she got out with as much conviction as she could muster. 'The situation would never arise.'

Liar, she accused herself. The situation has already arisen, was at this moment playing out like a scene from a torrid movie, and she was at once exhilarated and yet afraid.

'So convinced,' Todd chided, 'and so sure of yourself and Kel's fidelity.'

'Absolutely.'

'OK. We've established that as a happily married woman you uphold the sanctity of marriage.'

Kris frowned, glancing at him sharply. What was that in his tone, the slight mockery? Did he know...?

'Then just suppose——' Todd's voice brought Kris out of her deliberations '—that you and I, out here alone in the wilderness, decided we were physically attracted to each other.'

Kris opened her mouth, but he held up his hand.

'Hypothetically, of course,' he finished, holding her gaze.

Kris felt herself grow hot again in the cooling air, felt the urge to peel off the thick material of the overalls, have the night air temper the feverishness of her burning skin.

All systems flashed danger, senses Kris hadn't even been aware she possessed in her make-up, and she knew she had to defuse the rising tension his provocative words were inciting.

'Then it would be no go, unfortunate though it might be for both of us.' She gave him what she hoped was a regretful smile. 'Trust has to work both ways.'

He watched her, like a spider trying to will its victim into its web, and Kris ran a hand around the back of her neck, lifting the slightly damp tendrils of her hair to the fresh evening air.

Then he gave a soft, harsh laugh. 'You make it sound so easy.'

'And you make it sound so difficult,' Kris countered. 'That's the trouble with cynics.'

'Cynics?' He turned those glittering eyes on her. 'Perhaps. But in this case I would have said simply a realist.'

Kris clamped her teeth on an angry retort, convinced he expected just that. 'Then obviously you haven't met the right person yet,' she made herself say evenly, knowing she sounded unsophisticatedly trite.

His eyes moved over her face, held her gaze, and Kris had to shift her position again to disguise the shiver that crept seductively up her spine.

'Perhaps I haven't,' he said softly, and Kris's bones went to water. 'But I live in hope.'

She shot a quick glance at him to see if he was mocking her again. Her lips thinned. No doubt that hope had gained him a lot of experience during his search. Well, Kris had no intention of joining the queue of hopeful women who stayed a while and were banished when he tired of them.

'But don't worry, Kris. I haven't lost any sleep over it.' He grinned. 'Sorry. Wrong choice of words there.'

'But I can believe it,' Kris said with feeling, before she could prevent herself.

'Oh?' His dark brows went up. 'Now what could you mean by that, Mrs Quade?'

'I've seen some photos of you in the newspapers; you're not often alone.' Kris tried to keep her tone light, teasing, wishing she felt as easy.

'You don't want to believe everything you see and read in the newspapers. Mostly media hype, I can assure you.' His deep voice assaulted her senses again.

Kris gave a thin, nervous laugh. 'Well, I'm sure you don't care what I think about you. You don't even know me.'

'No? But we're in the ideal situation to get to know each other, aren't we?'

'To a degree, I suppose,' Kris acknowledged carefully, 'but the situation isn't a normal one. It's... well——' she stumbled over finding the right words '—it's sort of larger than life, I guess. Out of perspective.'

And that's just what he was to her at the moment, she told herself. Far larger than life. And therefore not to be taken at face value. Their circumstances were critical and so their instincts were honed to fine pitch in a deep primeval bid for survival. Weren't they all the best ingredients for total over-reaction?

No wonder his fabulous looks, the magnetism of the man had taken on such importance. Under normal circumstances she'd have looked, admired momentarily, and gone on her way. And did she really believe that? jeered an inner voice.

Kris glanced across at Todd Jerome and her heart did an unusual flutter in her chest, like a butterfly caught in a net.

She *had* to believe it! She wasn't interested in starting a relationship with anyone, least of all an attractive, high-profile, physical animal like this man. He was way out of her league and she knew it.

'Out of perspective,' he repeated softly and Kris glanced at him. 'Do you always keep both feet so firmly on the ground, Biggles?'

'Well, I try to.' Kris stifled the irritation his words sparked. He made her feel insipid and downright dull. 'However, I'm hardly a child any more. I'm afraid I can't get away with frivolous, immature behaviour.'

'Twenty-six isn't walking-stick time, you know,' he said drily. 'And what's wrong with enjoying your life?'

'I do,' Kris admitted. 'What makes you think I don't? Because I'm not a social butterfly? A perpetual party-goer?'

He watched her and she had the feeling that he was trying to see down into her soul, into the secret recesses of her being.

Her gaze fell. She didn't want those all-seeing eyes to peel away her protective coating. She was already more than vulnerable enough where he was concerned.

'And do you ever have any fun, Biggles?' he asked, and his resonant voice seemed to stop the rustle of the dry leaves in the scrubby trees nearby.

'Fun?' Kris folded her dry tongue around the word. 'Of course I do,' she stated shortly.

He continued to watch her and her hand went unconsciously to her throat to hide the tell-tale pulse that throbbed there.

'You don't have to party till you drop every night to have fun,' Kris added derisively.

'I suppose not.' Silence fell between them again until eventually he broke its heavy thickness. 'Have you lived all your life on the station?'

'Most of it,' Kris said, wary at his change of subject. 'I worked in Townsville for a few years.' She gazed into the darkness.

After Kel died she'd made herself do extensive training in computers and had even taken a position teaching her subject. 'But I went back to Amaroo to help out last year when my uncle's housekeeper left,' she finished. And she'd suddenly and inexplicably needed the safety of her family. The loneliness of the city had begun to weigh down on her and she'd bolted for home.

'I suppose it's difficult getting staff to stay for long on an isolated property,' Todd put in and Kris nodded.

'Yes. Amaroo is quite a way out,' she acknowledged, and Todd gave a soft laugh again.

'I suppose that was the reason the charming Donna omitted to tell me precisely where I would have to go to give her the financial advice she said she and her cousin, you, needed so desperately.'

'We will be inheriting some investments from our grandmother,' Kris assured him quickly, should he suspect Donna's real purpose for luring him out to Amaroo.

'I'm relieved to hear it,' he remarked drily, 'but by the way Donna spoke of Amaroo it would have been a fair assumption on my part to imagine I could have walked out there.'

'Distances are judged differently in the outback,' Kris defended her cousin. 'Did Donna tell you much about herself?' Kris paused. 'About us?'

He shook his head. 'In retrospect, not much, although she seemed to do a lot of talking. Her husband's overseas at present, I take it?'

'In the States on business. They're very happily married,' Kris added and then flushed. Would he realise she was warning him off?

'I'm sure they are.' His eyes met and held hers.

Kris's gaze fell and she swallowed, his slightly mocking expression disconcerting her. She adjusted her position and to her consternation she knocked the lantern.

His hands reached out as hers did and they caught the falling light between them, his fingers covering hers for seconds that stretched to what seemed like an eternity, and Kris's heartbeats began to thunder in her breast. It took all of her shaky concentration not to snatch her hands from his.

He released her and she was totally incapable of meeting his eyes for fear that he'd see the effect his touch had had on her. As she set the lantern more safely on the packing case she heard him catch his breath as he moved.

'Is your leg giving you trouble?' she asked, her voice only slightly thin to her ears.

'Let's just say I know it's there,' he said with a crooked smile and Kris frowned.

'Shall I have a look at it?'

'It's OK. Just a little stiff now those pills you gave me have worn off.'

'I'll get you some more.' Kris went to get up, but he stopped her.

'No. Don't worry, Kris. It's not that bad. A good sleep should work wonders.'

'If you're sure.'

He nodded. 'I'm sure. And talking of sleep, I guess we should be getting some.' With that same crooked smile he motioned for her to join him on the rug.

Kris came suddenly awake and she blinked into the heavy darkness until she remembered where she was. Out in the bush. Stranded. With Todd Jerome. Her body tensed as she felt the warmth of his arm against hers and she lay still, trying to identify what had woken her.

There was no sound save the usual quiet of the night and she strained for some alien noise that might have disturbed her.

Then she suddenly became aware of the stillness in the man beside her and she knew instinctively that he was also awake.

'Todd?' His name came softly, naturally from her lips, and her hand went to the solidness of his arm.

'Did I disturb you, Kris? I'm sorry.'

'It's your leg, isn't it?' She raised herself on one elbow and reached for the lantern, bathing them in shadowy light.

'It's OK,' he said shortly. 'Put that darn thing out and go back to sleep.'

Kris sat up and moved the lantern closer to the man beside her. 'It's not all right and you know it. I can tell by your voice.'

She reached out and put her hand on his forehead. It was cool, but slightly damp. 'How long has it been like this?'

He sighed loudly. 'Florence Nightingale again, Biggles?'

Kris drew a deep breath, ready to retaliate, but he continued before she could comment.

'It started to ache a little after lunch, but it's grown worse since we turned in. Might be a little infection there.'

Kris set her lips, feeling a rising panic clutch at her. She was no doctor and the first-aid kit, although adequate, was hardly up to a major medical crisis.

'I'll get you some more pain-killers.'

'No, Kris. I don't want them. It's not unbearable and it will be light in an hour or so. Let's leave it until we're able to see it properly.'

'But...' Kris bit her lip. 'Are you in much pain?'

'Only when I laugh, Biggles, so no telling smutty jokes.'

'This is hardly the time for jokes of any kind, wouldn't you say?' Kris felt like hitting him. 'Look, are you sure? About the pain-killers, I mean?'

'I'm positive,' he reiterated firmly. 'Now lie down and try to get some sleep for what's left of the night.'

Well, she could hardly force-feed him the tablets, Kris told herself irritably as she switched off the lantern and settled back into the blackness that surrounded them once again.

It seemed so much quieter now, almost vacuous, and she couldn't suppress a shiver.

'Cold?'

His deep voice made her jump.

'Just a little from moving, I guess.'

'Lift your head.'

'What?' Kris turned to face him in the dark, but could only make out the chiselled outline of his so perfectly hewn profile. 'Why?'

He shifted beside her and she knew by the careful way he did it that his leg was definitely causing him discomfort. His hand went out and he gently lifted her head, sliding his arm beneath her neck, settling her back into the crook of his arm.

She fitted perfectly, as though she had always been meant to be there, nestled against him. Yet even as part of her mind recognised that fact her cautious body was stiffening at his touch.

Todd gave a soft laugh. 'I told you no jokes, Biggles.'

'I didn't... I don't recall saying anything even slightly amusing,' she got out, feeling as though every muscle in her body had stretched as tautly as a guitar string. And every nerve-ending was chiming an excited, alarmed, totally dismayed melody.

'You didn't have to say anything,' he said lightly. 'Your body language did all the talking.'

'Really?' Kris prompted. 'Well, you're wrong. I assure you I don't feel in the least amused.'

'No? I do. I mean, I think the suggestion of my starting a seduction at this particular moment is downright hilarious.'

Inside Kris was a mass of quivering sensations. And each and every one of them clamoured for just that. Seduction.

Seduction? She repeated the word in her mind. It had the sound of soft allurement in it. And gentleness. But she didn't feel gentle. Her burning body was on fire for him. Seduction. Ravishment. Call it by any name. There was no denying she wanted him. Desperately. And he would certainly laugh if he knew.

'No one mentioned seduction, Mr Jerome.' Kris was amazed at the even tone of her voice and she managed to draw a harsh gulp of air into her aching lungs. 'But I don't doubt it's a word you know all about,' she threw at him, her self-disgust, self-castigation adding a sneer to her words.

'Ahh!' He expelled a soft breath that fanned the hair above her temple and her traitorous body responded accordingly, devastatingly.

Kris wanted to move away from him, but she rather suspected she wouldn't be able to should her life depend on it.

'That, my dear Kris, sounded remarkably like a challenge. Now, what red-blooded Australian male would be able to refuse such an obvious throwing down of the gauntlet?'

'I did no such thing!' Kris stormed, turning to face him.

Not the best defensive manoeuvre, she realised immediately. In fact, it was a grave tactical error, because it placed her lips in the exact vicinity of his. And, try as she might, as she knew she should, she couldn't, or rather wouldn't evade the downward movement of his head.

His mouth made soft, oh, so gentle contact with hers, retreated tortuously, then miraculously returned to slide with practised slowness, touching, inflaming every last responsive millimetre, until her entire body was gripped by a desire so strong that she felt faint. She heard herself groan huskily, raspily, deep in her throat.

And the hoarse sound seemed to ignite the flame in him for his teasing gentleness was replaced by a burning hunger as fiery, as all-consuming as her own.

CHAPTER FOUR

HIS other hand came around her, fingers splayed out across her midriff, just below her breasts, searing her skin through the thick material of her overalls.

Without any conscious direction on her part Kris's hand slid up his arm, feeling the mound of hard muscle beneath his thin shirt, slipped over his shoulder, stole around to the nape of his neck until her wayward fingertips were lost in the soft vitality of his dark hair. It felt so good. His hair. His skin. His lips on hers. The taste of him.

The fire blazed in them both, their hands on each other's bodies fanning the flames, until it raged out of control, threatening to consume them with its intensity.

Todd's lips left hers to move across her cheek, then continued downwards to settle at the base of her throat, where her pulse throbbed, raced with an erratic lack of self-control.

He made to move his body closer to her and the sound of his gasp of pain as he jarred his injured leg filtered slowly through Kris's almost mindless arousal, the sound as effective as a clanging warning bell.

She stilled, coming back down to earth with an almighty thud that made her go cold where a mere second ago she had been burning hot. What was she doing? What was she allowing him to do?

Her hand went to his shoulder, pushing frantically, but with little pressure or purchase. Her muscles, her bones were still lifeless, uncoordinated. However, the movement was enough to evoke a silent stillness in the man beside her.

'Please.' The word came out of her bruised lips and, hearing it, Kris herself couldn't decide whether it was a plea or a rejection. She gathered her failed defences together with a mammoth effort. 'Please, Todd. Let me go.'

His arms held her fast, making no move to do as she bid him.

'Todd, I can't... This is madness. We shouldn't...' Kris stuttered impotently.

'But it feels so right,' he said, his voice laced with obvious sarcasm.

Kris's teeth clamped together as an almost welcome anger replaced the other terrifying emotion that had very nearly been her undoing. 'Don't be ridiculous,' she bit out, and he gave a sharp laugh.

'Ridiculous! It felt anything but ridiculous, I assure you,' he replied with ominous quietness as he rolled slowly on to his back, one hand still holding her in the crook of his arm. 'But I guess you're right, Mrs Quade. It was a moment of madness, one I'm sure that even an indulgent husband wouldn't understand.' He paused for long seconds. 'You being such a happily married woman, that is,' he finished with heavy sarcasm.

'Please. Don't!' Kris's voice caught and she heard the man beside her mutter an oath beneath his breath.

'Oh, for heaven's sake!' he growled abruptly. 'There's no harm done. Your slight misdemeanour won't be written on your forehead for the world to see, so let's not conduct a post-mortem on the ''fors and againsts'' right now. Shall we simply forget it happened and try for some sleep before the sun comes up?'

Sleep? Was he serious? Kris wanted to shout at him. How could they simply put those tension-filled, emotive moments behind them as though they'd never happened and calmly relax and sleep? He had to be joking!

Kris's body felt as though all her muscles had locked and her pulse continued to race, pounding inside her like a death knell at triple time. She suspected she'd never be able to sleep again. Yet surprisingly she did. After a while her tense muscles eased, her eyelids drooped, and she drifted into a yearned-for unconsciousness, blissfully oblivious to the fact that she turned instinctively towards Todd Jerome, her arm going across his chest, her breath escaping on a peaceful sigh.

Kris stirred. The sun was up over the ridge and she knew it was later than she usually awoke. Then she became conscious of the warmth beside her and she stiffened as the events that had occurred before dawn came flooding back to her.

She couldn't have kissed Todd Jerome with such terribly wanton abandon... could she? Then why was she cradled in his arms, as though she had been born to be there?

Slowly she moved apart from him, freezing as his arms tightened momentarily and then relaxed. She waited a while and moved again until she eventually slid undetected from their makeshift bed.

For long moments she stood gazing down at him, a kaleidoscope of emotions flitting through her. In repose he looked far too vulnerable, his dark hair falling over his forehead, those firm lips slightly apart. Inviting.

Kris turned angrily on her heel and walked on shaky legs to the crashed aeroplane, putting it between herself and the so dangerous Todd Jerome. She groaned softly and rested her burning forehead against the cooler metal surface of the plane.

What had happened here? In—what? Could it be less than two days? Admittedly she had found him attractive, but he was also the most unbearably chauvinistic man she had ever had the misfortune to meet. He still was. The crash couldn't have changed him so radically. And she had never been a push-over for a handsome face in the past. So why now?

Proximity, she told herself. It was all due to the fact that they had been thrown together in a critical situation. If they'd met out in the street in ordinary circumstances she'd never have fallen in love with him.

In love with him? Kris blanched. Love had nothing to do with it. It was all physical. She was attracted to him and... Well, it had been over four years since... She was a normal, healthy woman. It was hormones, she told herself firmly. Yet she knew the disquietude of a very real element of doubt.

'Kris!' The sound of her name jarred the morning air, severing her fanciful thoughts, and she felt every nerve, every muscle in her body go on alert.

'Kris!'

She had to move, but somehow she couldn't. She wasn't ready to face him. Not yet.

His shadow warned her he was approaching and she had time to draw one steadying breath before his large frame came into view. He stopped dead when he saw her and he was so obviously angry.

'Why the hell didn't you answer me?' he demanded, his hand going out to the plane to steady himself.

'I...' Kris drew another breath. 'I'm sorry. I only just heard you.'

His eyes impaled her in disbelief. 'I've been shouting for hours. I'll be surprised if they haven't heard me in Townsville.'

'Well, *I* didn't hear you,' Kris repeated shortly. 'I was—well, I was thinking about...' She stopped. About you. She'd rather die than admit that to this man, this self-composed, so sure of his own attraction Todd Jerome.

'About?' He raised one eyebrow sardonically.

'About the plane. About fixing the radio. About us getting out of here,' she finished angrily and brushed past him. 'And about your leg. Do you want me to look at it before or after we've eaten?' she threw over her shoulder.

When she reached the small fireplace they had fashioned she knelt down and lit the fire beneath the container of water before turning to face him again. He was limping badly and the expression on his face was thunderous.

'So true to your vocation, Florence Nightingale.' His voice mocked her with his usual acidity.

'You should be thankful I am,' Kris told him. 'It would serve you right if I left you to it, wound and all.'

Surprisingly he sighed and sat down on the packing case. 'Just don't wander off, Kris. Anything could have happened to you.'

Kris knew there was some truth in what he said. 'All right. I see your point and I'm sorry I got angry with you but——'

'But?' he prompted.

'Let's just say you rub me the wrong way.'

'That could be considered debatable in——' he paused '—some quarters,' he finished softly and Kris stiffened, feeling colour wash her face.

The man had no shame. 'And that comment is pretty typical.'

'Meaning?' he asked with a frown.

'I don't think I need to elaborate.'

'Humour me,' he said, his heavy sarcasm once more in evidence.

'It means I don't care to discuss it and I think we should see to your wound,' Kris replied with far more aplomb than she was feeling. 'Now, I'll just fetch the first-aid kit. By then the water will be hot.'

He muttered irascibly under his breath as Kris headed back to the plane.

He was the most annoying... But if only he weren't so attractive...

Pull yourself together, Kris admonished herself. Usually she was self-possessed, stable, well-adjusted, in control of herself and her life.

She took a deep breath. And she still was. There. Now she had her sense of proportion back and she could look at Todd Jerome in the right context, as simply a better-than-average-looking man.

But the feelings of uneasiness were overshadowed by the sensations of purely sensual longing that Todd's kisses, his caresses had stirred within her obviously not so dormant body in the enveloping darkness of the early morning. And it seemed they hadn't been extinguished by the harsh reality of daylight.

Tingles rose from the pit of her stomach and she groaned inwardly as she gave herself some stern, self-derogatory orders under her breath.

Resolutely she collected the first-aid kit and walked purposefully back to join him. Eventually she had to raise her eyes from the dry, dusty ground and it was just as well that he was engrossed in unwinding the bandage from his leg for Kris's step faltered at the sight of him, her knees going to water, and she all but stumbled.

His shirt was open, revealing the light mat of dark hair on his muscular chest, and he'd removed his trousers. All Kris's carefully built good intentions cracked and began to crumble.

He'd finished removing his bandage now, displaying the jagged wound.

Kris took another step forward. 'How is it?' she asked, miraculously finding her voice as she stood watching him, fervently hoping he wouldn't see and recognise the emotions she felt sure were reflected in her green eyes.

'Not as bad as I was expecting,' he replied without looking up. 'There's a little inflammation, but maybe the aching was only the bandage being slightly tight.'

'I'll bathe it and rebandage it.' Kris turned and picked up the first-aid kit. Her fingers fumbled and it slipped from her hand to clatter to the ground.

Todd Jerome watched her through narrowed eyes. 'What's the matter, Nurse Nightingale? Not going to do a shrinking violet on me, are you?'

'Of course not. Can't I drop something without you holding a full enquiry?' Kris regathered the kit and promptly dropped it again.

'Fiddle-fingered *and* touchy. What's caused this, Biggles? Had a bad night, hmm?'

'No, I didn't have a bad night,' Kris got out between clenched teeth. 'And any normal, reasonably well-mannered man wouldn't sit there in next to nothing making snide insinuations.'

'Ahh! So that's it. The sight of my male body unnerves you.'

'You are by far the most unchivalrous——'

'Oh, undoubtedly unchivalrous,' he agreed mockingly. 'So just in case my more primal instincts get the better of me are there any smelling-salts for my lady in that damned first-aid kit, should she faint dead away, that is?'

Kris felt her face diffuse with angry colour. She should have stuck by her first impressions. He was the rudest, crudest——

'Tell me, Biggles. Where the hell have you been all your life? I thought Victorian maidens went out as the Pill came in. Next thing you'll be telling me good old Kel never appeared without modest covering and that you only ever made love in the dark.'

'Where and how Kel and I made love is hardly any of your business,' Kris annunciated with ominous quietness. 'And as I've told you before I've no intention of discussing such a subject with you. You're just a rude, coarse, uncouth ocker and——'

Todd Jerome held up his hand. 'OK, I get the picture, Mrs Quade. No need to expand on it. I'm sorry if I offended you, but to tell you the truth I'm just not in the mood for any maidenly outrage over my present state of dress. My leg hurts like hell, so could we simply get it over with so I can cover myself up again and save you any more undue indignity?'

In portentous silence Kris fetched the hot water and attended to his leg, making herself put her anger aside.

At last it was done and she could pack everything away. She handed him a couple of pain killers and he took them without a word, sighing as he slipped back into his light cotton trousers and sat back on their make-shift bed.

Once they'd eaten Todd informed her he was going to take another look at the radio and they spent most of the morning working silently if not companionably in the far too close confines of the upturned aircraft. As much as Kris would have liked to deny it, the heady tension hung between them like smoke haze in a dingy basement disco.

'That should be it. Give it a try now,' Todd said as he sat back and handed Kris the mouthpiece.

Kris took a deep breath and flicked the switch. 'Mayday. Mayday. This is Victor Hotel Sierra. Do you read me, Townsville?'

She listened intently, but there was no reply. 'I got some static. It's faint, but...' She shrugged and tried again before sitting back dejectedly. 'No go, I'm afraid.'

'I think there's every chance we're putting out a signal even if we're not receiving,' Todd said, running a hand through the thickness of his dark hair.

Desperately Kris clung to the hope—a faint hope, she knew, but a hope nevertheless. 'Want to break for a cup of tea?' she asked him and he nodded.

'I'll keep at this.' He indicated the ailing radio and Kris climbed from the cockpit.

She was about to pour boiling water into their mugs when she thought she heard the drone of an engine.

It was half a minute before she could move. Her mind told her she'd heard the sound, but her muscles simply refused to take instruction. Staggering to her feet, she raced for the survival kit, gathering up the piece of mirror she'd left at hand for just such a development.

'Todd!' she called and he stuck his head through the open cabin door. 'I heard a plane. I'm sure I did.'

'Which direction?' he asked as he cocked his head to listen.

'I don't know.' Her eyes feverishly scanned the clear blue sky, her ears straining for that same sound, but she heard nothing. Kris swallowed. Could she have been mistaken, imagined that faint, steady hum? No, she was sure she hadn't. Where had it come from? Her head turned agitatedly from left to right.

'You take the mirror to the top of the ridge. You'll be able to get a better view from up there,' Todd bade her. 'I'll try the radio again.'

Kris was galvanised into action, running as fast as she could up the rise, her trainers slipping on the stony ground. As she topped the ridge she stopped, drawing painful gulps of air into her burning lungs.

Please, God, don't let me have missed them. She began to chant the words over and over inside her head.

No. There it was again, that faint, far-off buzzing. It had to be a plane. She brought up the mirror, angling it to catch the sun, sending the flash in the direction of the sound, hoping to catch the attention of what had to be their means of rescue.

How long she kept up the signal she couldn't later have told, for the time stood still. She moved forward, willing the plane to turn in their direction. But it didn't. And then it was gone.

Kris let her hands fall to her sides, her knees folding under her as she sank down on to the hot, rocky ground.

They hadn't seen her. They couldn't have. Otherwise they would have changed course to investigate.

Two large tears welled in her eyes, overflowed to cascade down her warm cheeks, as she wept with disappointment and fear.

Would they never be found? Were they fated to die in this hot, inhospitable land, leaving their families to suffer the loss of hope, the torment of not knowing what had actually become of them?

Kris's tears continued to flow. She couldn't seem to stop them. Or want to stop them. She sat with her arms resting on her raised knees, her head falling on to her arms, and she cried. The dam of shock and worry she'd held back since the crash broke and proceeded to engulf her.

But at last she raised her head and drew a deep, quivering breath, wiping the dampness from her face with the sleeve of her overalls. She couldn't just sit here and wallow in negative thoughts, she tried to tell herself. She had to be positive, remain confident, optimistic.

With a derisive smile she stood up, turned on her heel, and walked back over the ridge, only to stumble to a halt on the stony ground as she saw Todd making his painful way up the rock-strewn incline, using a thick stick as a cane.

'Where the hell have you been all this time? You were supposed to go to the top of the hill and flash the signal, not follow the bloody plane to Townsville.' He straightened, long legs apart, his free hand aggressively on his hip. 'Every time I turn my back you disappear like the proverbial magician's rabbit.'

'I wanted to wait until I was sure they'd really gone.'

'And I don't suppose you saw any need to tell me your intentions instead of simply doing another vanishing act?' His words cut across hers.

'I thought you were trying the radio and that you, in turn, would keep on trying the damn radio.' Kris shrugged exaggeratedly. 'My abject apologies, but——' she began caustically.

'Your apologies? Didn't it cross that selfish little mind of yours that I might be just a trifle worried if you didn't return after a reasonable amount of time, that I might have suspected you'd done a tumble down the cliff or something?' he threw at her just as sarcastically.

'Will you stop cutting in on everything I try to say?' Kris's own anger blossomed. It was too much to take, coming so close upon missing the first plane to come within 'cooee' of them. 'If you'd only stop thumping your chest like some phoney Tarzan in a low-budget movie I'd be able to——'

'Phoney Tarzan!' he bit out, the words menacingly low-toned, as he took a measured pace forward.

Kris's first reaction was to back away up the hill, but she made herself hold her ground. She had no intention of letting Todd Jerome intimidate her or of ending up undignifiedly on her backside on the slippery hillside.

She made herself hold his gaze and walked carefully forward and around him.

'Thin ice, Biggles. You're treading on very thin ice,' he said, regarding her through narrowed eyes as she passed him.

In an oppressive silence they made their way down to the crash site, Todd relying on his makeshift cane on the loose stony surface. They were both fraught with disappointment, Kris knew, and she should try to defuse their angry confrontation.

With a sigh she turned back to face him. 'Look, I stayed up on the hillside to give the plane every chance to see the signal,' she explained reasonably. 'I knew you couldn't make it up there as quickly with your leg. I know how painful it is and——'

'It's only a minor wound, for heaven's sake.' He made a sweeping gesture with his arm.

'Sounds more like a wounded ego to me,' Kris muttered under her breath before she could stop herself, and then she did take a step backwards as his head went up, his jaw thrust towards her.

'Would you care to repeat that?' he invited quietly.

'No.' Kris's mouth was suddenly dry.

Todd took another deliberate step forward. 'No? No grit all of a sudden, Biggles? You disappoint me.'

'All I said was you sounded as though you had a dented ego,' Kris was stung into replying.

'So says Mrs Quade, the woman of the world. That's a very credible opinion from someone who was married from the cradle and who's barely seen past the boundary of a cattle station,' he taunted.

'It seems to me,' Kris said with dignity, 'that everything's all right with your world as long as you're calling the shots. When you can't boss everyone around you get belligerent and——'

He was on her in one long stride and his hand grasped her arm above the elbow with bruising pressure.

Kris swallowed, trying not to let him see that his expression was deflating some of her earlier bravado. 'Let go of my arm. You're hurting me,' she threw at him. 'I'm beginning to think you're nothing but a brute and a bully.'

'Oh, very flattering, Biggles. I'd quit while I was ahead if I were you,' he said through clenched teeth.

'Let me go!' Kris tried to squirm from his vice-like grip, to no avail. 'This disgraceful behaviour might go down well with the sort of women you're used to in the city, but up here in the country men don't force themselves on women after they've been knocked back.'

'Ah!' He slowly released her and she took a couple of steps backwards, away from him, some measure of relief washing over her.

'Now we're getting past the pleasantries and down to the basics.' He shifted his stick from one hand to the other. 'So that's what you think is behind my ill humour.' A slow smile that held no humour lifted the corners of his mouth. 'There's nothing like a bout of sexual frustration to make a man behave like a—what was it? A brute and a bully?' he mocked. 'You must read some illuminating and racy books, Biggles.'

'Don't be crude.'

'But that's what you seem to expect from city guys, isn't it?' he said disdainfully, taking a deliberate step towards her. 'We're so far removed from your good old chivalrous country boys.'

'I didn't say...' she began, and couldn't prevent herself taking an involuntary step away from him again. Her eyes were locked with his and she wanted to run for safety. And stay to know the heady danger.

'Don't move, Kris!' His change of tone held her momentarily motionless before her lips twisted.

'If you think I'm going to take orders from you you're very much mistaken,' she stated and spun defiantly on her heel. And then she froze, her blood turning to ice in her veins.

There on the gravelly ground, about six feet in front of her, was a long brownish-coloured snake. Her movement had obviously alerted it and it watched her stilly, only its tongue moving agitatedly in and out of its mouth.

Kris felt a sliver of hysteria rise inside her. She hated snakes, had a real phobia about them. She couldn't so much as bear the thought of them. And now she faced one...

The streak of panic ballooned and she caught her breath, knowing she would be unable to simply stand there and watch the creature and wait.

'I can't... I don't think...' she whispered hoarsely, and then everything seemed to happen at once.

The snake reared slightly and came forward and Todd seemed to spring around Kris's paralysed body.

Kris closed her eyes, too terrified to scream. When she found the courage to open them again Todd had used his stick to fling the snake out of harm's way.

He came limping back towards her, his expression grim. 'I don't know much about snakes, but I think it was a common brown variety. We must have had the bad luck to get between it and its nest. As a precaution, I suggest we move our crates before nightfall in case it returns.'

Kris could only continue to stand where she was, still in a state of shock.

'Are you all right?' he asked and she tried to nod, but suddenly she had begun to shake.

He covered the space between them to take her in his arms, pulling her gently to his taut body. She put her hand on his chest, part of her knowing she should ward him off, but once she encountered the security of the hard wall of his midriff her feeble resolutions cracked and fell away and she almost collapsed against him.

'It's all right now,' he murmured, his breath teasing her hair, his arms supporting her sagging body.

'Thank you,' she got out with a shudder. 'I just can't abide snakes.'

'Most people can't,' he said soothingly.

Her cheek was resting against the warm, hard muscles beneath his shirt and suddenly her heartbeats were falling all over themselves in trepidation, in traitorous anticipation. The tension rose, was so thick about them that Kris could almost taste it.

She had to do something. Make a move... Yet all she really wanted was to remain exactly where she was. Forever.

Taking a faltering breath, she leant backwards, put a little space between them. 'I'm sorry you had to...to...' She grimaced distastefully.

'No trouble.' His gaze met hers, held her immobile, and the ember that had glowed about them sparked to life in a blaze of desire. Kris watched it flare in the depths of his eyes and she knew the fire was reflected in her own.

She closed her eyes as his lips came down to claim hers.

CHAPTER FIVE

KRIS'S lips opened beneath the pressure of his, dissolved as his kiss deepened and he explored the sweetness within.

It was a kiss unlike any she'd experienced before. Even Kel... A faint niggle of uneasiness impinged on her consciousness, but her aroused senses at this moment in time refused to give it consideration.

Kel. She had to make herself think. And that was totally impossible to do as his lips bewitchingly ravaged her senses.

His mouth surrendered hers and they both drew deep, steadying breaths. Kris fought for control and when he would have lowered his head once more she gasped his name.

'Todd, don't...'

'Don't? Oh, but I want to. And I have a gut feeling you want to, too.'

'No. I don't.' Kris swallowed. 'Todd, this is wrong.'

'Wrong? Why do you say that?' His arms held her captive as he gazed scornfully down at her. 'Let me guess. Because we've just met. Or because you're a happily married woman.' His dark eyes challenged her. 'Well, you are, aren't you, Kris?'

'I...' Kris's vocal cords refused to work. If she was going to stand by that excuse she'd now have to lie blatantly. Could she?

'Oh, Kris. All pretext. You're no more married than I am, are you?'

Speechlessly, Kris gazed up at him.

'Donna said her cousin was a widow. That description doesn't fit cousin Christopher the pilot, so it has to be you, hasn't it, Cousin Kristle?'

'Even if it does that doesn't mean I'm . . . I want to . . . Just let me go,' she finished desperately.

'Let you go!' he repeated hoarsely and gave a soft throaty laugh that sent spirals of sensation surging along the entire length of Kris's body. 'Let you go. Right now I don't think I could if I wanted to.'

His eyes burned into hers and she knew risk and exhilaration warred inside her.

'And right now,' Todd continued, 'I don't care how many men you've happily married. There's no way you can honestly deny we've been fighting this since the moment we met.' His words ended on a low moan as he propelled her impossibly closer to his hard body.

'Todd, please . . .' Her plea didn't get past her lips as his mouth claimed hers again.

She did struggle against him, she assured herself later, but she wouldn't admit just how pathetic her resistance was. As his mouth covered hers she knew she was lost.

They clung together, lips to lips, breast to breast, hips to hips. And his body seared hers through their clothing. They might have been naked as they strained to get impossibly closer to each other. Passion flamed, consuming them, devouring them in its intoxicating blaze.

As Todd kissed her his fingers threaded through her hair, slid to her ears, her throat, over the creamy skin of her shoulders as he pushed the overalls aside.

And Kris helped him as she shrugged her arms from the sleeves before her own fingers began to unbutton his shirt with scant care for the thin white material and a button flew to be lost in the gravelly dust at their feet. But neither of them noticed.

Kris pulled his shirt from the waist of his trousers and tossed it aside, leaving his upper body bare. With a soft, husky moan of pleasure she ran her hands lightly over the smooth masculine contours, before following the provocative path of her fingers with her tongue-tip.

Todd's breath caught in his throat as he pulled her back against him, his hands unclasping her bra, letting the wisp of lace fall the way of his shirt.

'So beautiful!' he breathed hoarsely. His hands moulded the full curves of her breasts, his thumbs brushing the rosy peaks, and Kris's knees threatened to give way beneath her as a wave of purely erotic sensation washed over her.

With one pull the remaining press-studs on her overalls gave way and the loose garment fell over her hips. Kris stepped out of them as he reached for the cord at the waist of his beach trousers. The material caught on his bandage and with trembling hands Kris helped him undress.

He pulled her back into his arms, kissing her, his tongue tasting her, and she responded with a passion she hadn't known she was capable of. The scorch of his skin against hers drowned out any slight sound of caution her rational mind might have attempted as he lowered her on to the rug of their improvised bed, beneath the shade cover of the space blanket.

They strained together, fingers, tongues touching, teasing, tantalising.

Kris almost cried out as her body craved for fulfilment, wanting only to feel him moving with her. Now. Right now.

It was as though her senses had been honed, left primed since their embrace those few hours before, and it had only taken his touch to have those sensations leaping to all-consuming life. When his body loomed over her, cutting out the sun, she rose to meet him.

'God, Kris, I want to wait, but I don't think I can.' His dark hair had fallen forward over his brow and his grey eyes were dark pools in his flushed face.

'Don't stop. Please.' Kris heard the words, felt them escape from her lips, but she barely recognised her own voice.

His mouth claimed hers again. And he sank into her. Eagerly she went with him, drowning in an uncharted, delightful sea of pleasure before the wonder of ecstatic release.

All Kris's muscles seemed to have melted as she tried to catch her breath. It had been over in a second, or it had taken hours? She couldn't have told. She gulped air into her tortured lungs, scarcely believing in the reality of it. It had to have been a dream. A crazy, shameless, exquisite dream.

Todd moved then, stretching out beside her, and any thoughts, any hopes of fantasy shattered on to the hard, dusty ground around them.

'Kris?' There was a slight tentativeness in his voice as his breath fanned her ear, impossibly sending another fissure of sensation arrowing through her. 'Kris, I'm sorry. I...'

Was he going to apologise? She couldn't bear that.

He swore softly. 'I feel like a damn schoolboy. It was too quick.' He took an equally ragged breath and then his lips slid along the line of her jaw, found her mouth again, dropping tantalisingly soft kisses at each corner until her body arched against him again and she cried out his name.

'We'll go slowly this time,' he said as his fingers ignited the fire in her again with disconcertingly consummate ease.

This time their lovemaking was less feverish, a little less urgent, as they matched each other, instinctively seeking and finding each respective erotic place, until

they were both beyond control, elation lifting them
higher, catching them in a mutual delight.

Kris clung to him, repeating his name in a softly
languid litany. Through a sensual haze she heard herself
and a small part of her was shocked, totally astounded
by her complete recklessness, but she was incapable at
that moment of doing a thing about it. At that point in
time it appeared her own body was altogether out of her
hands. And entirely in Todd Jerome's.

'Oh, my God,' Kris whispered as they lay spent, bodies
still entwined, arms about each other. 'What have I
done?' She couldn't be sure she'd said the words out
loud, but it was her last conscious thought as she slipped
into an exhausted sleep.

The heat woke her. At least, her first sensation was
one of warmth. Her eyelids flickered open and then
closed to slits as the brightness of the noon sun assaulted
her eyes.

How long had she slept? She somehow had no impression of passing time. She went to lift her arm to
glance at her wristwatch, but her hand seemed to be
touching something... She moved her fingers and they
slid over firm, hot skin.

Kris's eyes opened wide, regardless of the dazzling
sunlight, and she raised her head from its comfortable,
commodious pillow.

In one blinding, comprehending flash she remembered where she was and why she was there. And with
whom. The realisation brought with it vivid memories,
flashing graphic pictures in to her mind, and with them
came a surge of that same sensual awareness. Kris
groaned in disbelief, in self-disgust.

She was lying on her side and her head had been tucked
into Todd's shoulder, her arm across his chest, one leg
twined with his. As though she'd been stung she drew

her arm away from its contact with Todd's hard body and her gaze shot upwards to meet his.

He was awake too, and he watched her, eyelids narrowed, his expression unfathomable.

'Good morning again,' he said softly and she felt the sound ripple tantalisingly, a soothing coolness over her hot skin. 'Or should I say, good afternoon?'

Kris swallowed and pushed herself up on one elbow, flushing as his eyes slid over the swell of her breast. She sat up, swinging away from him, her own eyes skittering of their own accord over the long masculine length of him.

He was really quite beautiful, part of her acknowledged reluctantly, his torso muscular yet well proportioned, tanned, apart from that one lighter strip where... Kris drew an agitated breath.

She had to be mad, she admonished herself. This couldn't be happening. Not to her. She couldn't have made love with this man, this virtual stranger. What had possessed her to do it? She had let blatant, purely physical sensations override her previously strong moral code.

Moral code! Kris groaned again and made to stand up, put as much space as she could between herself and the man beside her, but his fingers closed around her arm, holding her fast.

'Kris, we——'

'Let me go!' She slapped at his fingers. 'I want to...' She swallowed, trying to clear her tight throat. 'I want to get dressed.'

Her clothes lay with his on the dusty ground, in testimental disorder, left where they had carelessly discarded them. Just the sight of them filled Kris with even more self-revulsion.

Todd was sitting up beside her now and his breath fanned the back of her neck, sending shivers radiating outwards, downwards, tempting.

'Kris, we have to talk about this.'

'No.' She stood up, her back to him. 'I don't think we do,' she got out as she reached for her overalls. She could feel his eyes on her and she glanced angrily over her shoulder. 'Would you please have the decency to turn your back so I can get dressed? And get dressed yourself,' she added shortly.

'Avert my lecherous gaze?' he taunted lightly. 'Seems a little pointless, doesn't it? I mean, after I've——' he paused for obvious effect '—known your body so intimately.'

Kris fumed as hot colour flooded her cheeks. 'I might have known you'd make this whole situation even more impossible, more disreputable.'

'Disreputable? For heaven's sake, Kris. We're two consenting adults. It happened. We made love. If you'd admit——'

'Admit what? That I've just made one of the biggest mistakes of my life?' Clutching her overalls protectively in front of her, Kris spun to face him. Then she wished she hadn't.

Her eyes were drawn to the play of firm muscles as he slowly stood up, not attempting to cover himself, not in the least disconcerted by his nakedness. Her traitorous senses reacted instantaneously to the sheer sensuous sight of him and her anger intensified, rage directed at her own weakness warring with her erotic excitement.

'For God's sake, get dressed!' Kris picked up his cotton trousers and threw them at him.

He stood without moving as she struggled into her overalls. 'Are you always so shrewish after making love?' he asked with nettling sarcasm.

'That doesn't even deserve an answer.' Kris fought to keep calm. Her fingers were all thumbs as she tried to fasten the press-studs, cover her traitorous body. Her anger was affecting her co-ordination. That was what she told herself. 'And I'd appreciate it if we finished this conversation,' she added as evenly as she could, relieved to see he was pulling his trousers over his hips.

'Oh, you would, would you?' he replied quietly. 'End of subject. It never happened. How convenient.'

'Well, what do you suggest we discuss?' Kris yelled at him, exasperation and anger making her want to strike out at him. 'Should we dissect the whole show? Or maybe you want a rating or something?'

His lips had thinned and the stormy look in his eyes told her she'd succeeded in getting to him. The realisation spurred her on, made her light-headed with recklessness.

'We could compare notes, hmm? Now, let's see...' Kris struck a pose.

'That's not what I meant, Kris, and you know it.' His deep voice was softly ominous.

'Oh, come on, Todd. You've got an ego as big as a house.' Kris's smile was a travesty of humour. 'As a lover I'd give you eleven out of ten. I'm sure that's exactly what you want to hear. But as a man, I'm sorry, you don't rate at all.'

'Kris, you'd better leave it,' he began, but she forged onwards, the bit rashly between her teeth now.

'So what will you say about me, I wonder? I mean, when your brothers or the boys at the pub ask you what I was like?' Kris folded her arms, totally enjoying the livid set of his jaw, the fury in his eyes. 'Now you'll be able to tell them with complete honesty that I was a pushover, a real——'

'Cut it out, Kris!' The words escaped through his teeth. He was pale around his mouth, that same wonderful mouth that had set her aflame.

'It's the truth, isn't it?' she queried, not smiling now. 'I was easy prey for the great Todd Jerome, and once in your bed I was——'

He reached her in long strides, his hands gripping her arms as she held them out to fend him off. 'So it's ratings you want, is it? OK, Miss Holier-than-Thou. You were——' he paused, his eyes glittering in the bright light, impaling her, holding her gaze with the intensity of his, until long seconds later he finished his sentence '—pretty wonderful.' The words came out huskily, roughly, belying the cold anger in his face, in the tenseness of his body.

'And also, for the record, you were wrong again, Kris. I don't need to get my kicks giving my brothers or "the boys at the pub"——' he grimaced at the term '—blow by blow accounts of my indiscretions to prove anything, not to anyone else or to myself.' He drew a deep breath and his hold on her relaxed a little, although he didn't set her free. 'Now that we've settled that, can we discuss this like two rational adults?'

He continued to hold her gaze until she gave a faint nod.

'So.' His fingers released her and she made herself step back from him. 'We've just made love. Right here on that rug. In broad daylight. It happened, and pretending it didn't won't erase it,' he said with harsh honestly. 'So let's sort it out here and now.'

Kris bit her lip. 'But we shouldn't . . . It shouldn't have happened.'

'Maybe not. But it did.' His face was set enigmatically. 'And I'm afraid I can't say I'm sorry it did.'

Kris gave an exclamation of impatience as her bubbling anger resurfaced. 'Of course you're not sorry,' she threw at him. 'You got what you wanted. You were a success.'

'You didn't exactly lead me to believe you were finding it distasteful.' His hands were on his hips, his chin jutting aggressively. And the bright sunshine delineated the swell of his chest, highlighting each fine dark hair, the smooth masculine lines of him. 'I'd say it was a mutually satisfying affair, wouldn't you?'

Mutually satisfying? Kris had to bite back a tortured moan. If he only knew just how fulfilling it had been. But she wouldn't let him know. She couldn't.

'I can't deny you have an excellent technique,' she said as levelly as she could, 'but that's not everything.'

'Another compliment on my——' he paused '—performance?' One dark brow rose sardonically.

Kris flushed. 'That's not what I meant exactly. I meant...oh, I don't know what I meant,' she finished lamely, running an agitated hand through her tousled hair. 'I just wish we could turn back the clock, that's all.'

He stood regarding her with a suppressed tension that was evident in every line of his body. 'We can't do that, Kris,' he said in a low voice.

'Then we'll have to try to forget what...' Kris swallowed. 'Forget about it.'

He gave a short, harsh laugh. 'And will you be able to forget?'

'Yes. Yes, I will,' Kris repeated with more conviction than she actually felt. Who was she trying to kid? she asked herself. She had a sinking feeling she'd never be able to forget it, that she'd go on remembering for the rest of her life. That was the horrifying extent of it.

He folded his arms with slow mockery. 'And that will be it? Finished. Forgotten.'

'Yes,' Kris put in with as much conviction as she could muster.

'Well, I don't intend to forget, Kris,' he said quietly, ominously, and then bit off an angry oath. 'And you're a fool if you think *you* can.'

'If you had any decency——' Kris began, but he cut her off.

'You can paint me all colours of a heel in an effort to delude yourself into rationalising your own feelings, but it will all be just that. Delusions. We made love. And we both enjoyed it. More than enjoyed it.'

Kris shook her head.

'It's true, Kris. No matter what you say you think of me, you did enjoy it. Every last millimetre of you enjoyed it. The proof is there in the glow in your eyes, the soft curve of your mouth, the fullness of your lips.'

Kris caught her breath. 'You're despicable,' she choked out.

'Why? Because I'm honest? You should try it. Beginning with not lying to yourself.'

'I don't ... I haven't——'

'Oh, come on, Kris. For heaven only knows what reason, you're afraid of your own emotions. I can't even begin to guess what sort of marriage you had, but it can't have been much of a one.' He in turn ran his hand exasperatedly through his dark hair as Kris drew herself up to her full height.

'My marriage is none of your business,' she articulated clearly, fighting down a stab of untenable guilt. 'How can you possibly decide what sort of marriage I had when you never even met Kel? You don't know what he was like. And you don't really know me,' Kris bit out indignantly.

'Don't I?' He shrugged easily. 'I think I do. I know you're strong, independent, intelligent. You have a sense of humour, when you forget to pretend you're strait-laced and matronly. And I know you're the most sensual ...'

He took a breath and when he continued the tone of his deep voice dropped so that the words played over Kris's skin like an erotic melody. 'You're the most incredibly responsive woman I've ever met in my life. And if you were married to me we sure as hell wouldn't have the low-key, unexciting marriage you and Kel appear to have had,' he finished insolently.

'Unexciting?' Kris gasped, anger rising to wipe away the heady seduction of his earlier words. 'Why, you...' Kris drew a painful breath. 'That's unforgivable.'

'So deny it,' he put in smoothly. 'If you can.'

'I can and I will deny it. My marriage to Kel was wonderful.'

Todd took a step forward, his fingers clutching, biting into the soft flesh of her arms. 'Did he kiss you the way I kissed you? Make love to you the way I made love to you? Did he make you feel the way I made you feel?'

His eyes blazed angrily, arrogantly into hers before he crushed her to him. His mouth took hers, searing, punishing, plundering until she thought she'd faint dead away. Then his lips as suddenly surrendered hers.

'Why, you——'

He still held her arms and he shook her with restrained anger. 'Well, did he?' he persisted relentlessly. 'Be honest with yourself for once in your life, Kris.'

She held his gaze, unable to tear her eyes from the blazing emotion in the steely grey depths of his. The tense, taut silence stretched until it almost buzzed about them.

Kris swallowed. 'No,' she whispered, the word escaping from her tingling lips. 'No, Todd. Kel was gentle. Kind. Considerate. He was a wonderful... He loved me,' she finished on a half sob.

Slowly his punishing grip relaxed until his fingers released her, his hands dropping to his sides, and he stood before her, his face pale, his grey eyes narrowed in the relentless sunlight.

Kris watched him as a multitude of emotions battled inside her. She felt as though she was losing a grip on herself. Scenes from those moments of passion with Todd returned to taunt her as she tried desperately to hold on to her memory of Kel, his good-natured, smiling face.

But the image blurred, lost focus, was taken over by the ruggedly attractive lines of another face, by Todd Jerome's compellingly masculine features. And deep down a crazy, inexplicable yearning rose to almost engulf her, urging her to throw discretion to the wind, to confess to him that he was right, that Kel, that no man had ever touched her body, her soul the way he had, and that she'd like nothing more than to be part of his life. His days. And his nights.

Guilt and grief clashed with a heady physical need that burned again inside her. A tear, followed by another, overflowed to trickle down her hot cheek and she brushed at the dampness with the back of her hand. But before she could turn away his hand grasped her arm again, this time with uncharacteristic gentleness.

'Don't cry, Kris. Please.' His voice sounded hollow and throaty, as though it hurt him to speak, and she gazed up at him through a shimmer of tears. 'It doesn't show on your face, our having made love. No one will know.'

Kris shook her head resignedly. 'I'll know.'

'There's no need to torture yourself.' He muttered something under his breath that she couldn't catch. 'Perhaps you're right. We should just forget it ever happened.' His eyes narrowed as he looked down at her, his gaze settling on her lips for long, silent moments.

'It was a moment out of time.' His voice was softer, far more potently sensual, and his head seemed to be drawn downwards with slow deliberation, as though he couldn't prevent it.

And Kris made no move to avoid him. She could have turned away, and she knew he would have let her. But she didn't. At that moment she didn't want to stop him. She simply watched him, mesmerised. And waited.

Then his lips touched hers. Feather-soft. Lightly tantalising. She told herself she had to put an end to the rising tension, the heightened, steadily growing urgency. But of course it was far too late to return to rational thought. He could so easily take that clear-headed conception and toss it to the dry outback winds.

'I have my life,' he continued against her lips, his tone even softer, like liquid honey. And to Kris it tasted just as ambrosial, as temptingly sweet.

He kissed her again. And again. Tenderly, like whispers on a gentle breeze.

'And you have your life. This is all just time out of that life. Just time out,' he repeated softly, bewitchingly.

Those words played over Kris's mind and they shimmered inside her like heat waves dancing crazily in the hot blue summer sky. And they became interwoven with memories she couldn't quite recall.

She tried valiantly to grasp their significance. It had something to do with Kel. Kel. She'd wanted no one else. Had wanted. Past tense. It was time to let go, she tried to tell herself. Kel was her past. Todd Jerome was the future. And it terrified her.

But then Todd's drugging kisses deepened and she was totally lost as she melted into him, drowned in him.

They clung together, mindless of the heat of the sun beating down upon them, of the dry, dusty earth beneath their feet, of the faint rustle of the dry leaves in the scrubby bushes nearby. And of the swelling, throbbing sound that drew steadily closer.

CHAPTER SIX

THE alien noise increased from an indistinct buzz to the well-defined 'chop-chop-chop' of the rotor blades of a helicopter.

Todd and Kris slowly drew apart, both more than a little breathless, and it was long, lingering moments before the escalating sound encroached upon their private, isolated, so aroused world. Kris's hands remained resting against Todd's bare chest, still registering the heady, racing thump of his heartbeats, her eyes lost in the grey depths of his. As if disorientated, she languidly turned her head towards the sound.

Rescue. They were going to be rescued.

Suddenly she fell back to earth with a jarring thud. She was standing locked in Todd Jerome's arms. Other people were now intruding into this remote, secluded place. And they would be able to see... How would their embrace look to the rescue team in the chopper? Who could blame them for imagining the very worst?

Agitatedly she pushed away from Todd's body, but he held her fast. Her gaze swung to his and his still darkened eyes held, impaled hers for imperceptible seconds before slowly, deliberately, he set her free.

Kris stumbled backwards and then turned towards the approaching helicopter. She began to wave her arms frantically until she realised it was totally unnecessary, for they had obviously been seen.

The helicopter hovered above them and then moved sideways to a clear area some distance from them before beginning to descend. They had to protect their eyes as dust and grit and dry leaves flew about them until the rotor blades slowed.

But before they had stopped turning the door opened and the pilot stepped down, came towards them, his body bent forward, one hand holding his baseball cap on his head as the draught from the blades threatened to remove it.

He straightened and drew to a halt in front of them, holding out his hand. 'Kris Quade, I presume,' he said, a broad grin creasing his tanned and weathered face.

Kris took his hand and then he turned slightly. 'And Mr Todd Jerome.' He shook hands with Todd in turn. 'I'm Rick Lonergan. You've sure led us a merry dance, so am I pleased to see you two at last.'

'*You're* pleased to see *us*?' Kris repeated with feeling. She wanted to laugh and cry at the same time. 'We thought we were here for the duration. Especially after we missed that plane this morning.'

'You didn't miss them,' Rick told her cheerfully. 'That's how we came to be here. The search aircraft picked up a weak transmission from your radio, but they couldn't seem to get a message back to you. Luckily, while they were trying to pinpoint your position they saw your flashing signal.'

'We were afraid they hadn't seen us,' Kris told him as she recalled her disappointment.

'Unfortunately they had no way of acknowledging you because their fuel situation was critical. They were actually on their way back to base, but they did radio in your position and we came out as fast as we could. And here we are.' Rick Lonergan turned to indicate the helicopter and the man who must have climbed out of the aircraft behind him.

Only then did Kris realise there was someone else accompanying the pilot. An expensive-looking camera

covered the man's face and all Kris could see was a stock
of curling sandy hair.

The motor drive whirred before the man stepped
forward. He was about Todd's age, Kris now surmised,
not as tall, but his features were pleasantly attractive.

The man's gaze roved quickly over Kris before he
glanced at Todd, his grin broadening. 'You do have all
the fun, Todd,' he said easily.

The men shook hands and Todd grimaced. 'If you
could call it that,' he remarked drily and only when the
other man looked pointedly at Kris did Todd turn and
make the introductions. 'This is Matt Kane, a hack with
the *Courier Mail*.'

'Hack? Now that hurt,' he retaliated good-naturedly
as he took Kris's hand, holding it a little longer than
was necessary, a fact that did not go unnoticed by an
unsmiling Todd Jerome.

'I take it you two have met before.' Kris gently extri-
cated her hand, bringing an amused twinkle to Matt
Kane's eyes.

'Todd and I were at uni together—and don't take any
notice of him on my credentials. He has no taste. I'm
famous for my news-breaking stories, as well he knows.'

'Yes, I meant to phone you to thank you for that en-
lightened piece you ran last month,' Todd put in sardonically and Matt grinned again.

'One of my best. Very dramatic, I thought.'

'And full of——' Tod paused '—poetic licence.'

'Wait till you read the reports on the past few days.'
The newspaperman laughed. 'A couple more days out
here and they'd have made you a saint. You couldn't
have pulled a better political stunt if you'd contrived it.
And I'm giving you the benefit of the doubt that you
didn't.' He raised his fair eyebrows.

'Political stunt?' Kris whispered in disbelief, realisation of the implication of his words making her hackles

rise. 'Do you honestly believe all this——' she waved her arm at the crippled Cessna '—was a put-up job?'

'No. No.' Matt Kane held up his hand. 'Not at all, Miss Quade. Just a little joke between Todd and myself.'

'Misplaced humour,' Todd put in. 'And you've got some of your facts wrong, Matt. It's Mrs Quade.'

The fair eyebrows rose even higher as he glanced reflectively from Todd back to Kris.

'So how did you swing a seat on the chopper?' Todd indicated the helicopter with a wave of his hand. 'Not that I'm at all surprised to see you,' he added wryly.

'Rick owed me a small favour.' Matt shrugged affably, but before he could comment the pilot broke in on them.

'We should be making tracks. There's quite a welcome party waiting back at the airport.'

Kris looked down at her grubby overalls. 'I think I'll change back into my jeans, in the interests of the close confines of the helicopter cabin,' she said, wrinkling her nose. 'Unless that contraption over there——' she nodded at the aircraft '—comes with a nice hot shower.'

'Sorry. No can do on the shower.' Rick Lonergan laughed.

Matt Kane ran his eyes over Kris's offending outfit. 'Oh, I think we could have coped with the overalls, don't you, Rick? Very fetching, but I must admit it's hardly heroine attire.'

Kris laughed with him. 'Well, I'm afraid I'm hardly heroine material.'

'Oh, I don't know about that.' He gave her a mock leer. 'I know a genuine heroine when I see one, believe me.'

'Let's get moving, shall we?' Todd Jerome's deep voice cut into the light moment and Matt's eyes narrowed speculatively as he looked at the other man.

'Yeah. You're right, Todd,' agreed the pilot easily. 'Time's a-wasting. I'll just go and radio the base that you're safe and sound and in one piece.' He turned back to the helicopter and Kris started for the upturned Cessna.

'I could use fresh clothes, too, before you start to change.' Todd followed her, stooping to pick up his discarded shirt on the way, and Kris was glad she had her back to the newspaperman as hot colour flooded her face.

Would the journalist read anything into...? Oh, good grief! She admonished herself for her naïveté. If he was any sort of newspaper hound, which he most assuredly was, then he'd have the whole story in one. From high above, the pilot and the newspaperman couldn't have missed seeing her standing locked in Todd Jerome's embrace.

Kris strode around the other side of the plane and pulled open the misshapen cabin door, reaching inside for her clothes.

'You just might need this.' His deep voice came from behind her and she swung angrily towards him.

'I don't need anything from you...' The last word faded away as her gaze fell to his hand. Hooked over one finger by its strap was her lacy bra, swinging nonchalantly, denouncingly. Her teeth snapped shut on her fury.

His crooked smile was almost his undoing. Kris had never felt closer to physical violence in her life and she drew a deep, steadying breath before she snatched the offending garment from him.

'Thank you,' she said with careful contempt. 'How chivalrous of you, Mr Jerome.'

'That's me, Biggles. You know me so well. Although you could have put a little more feeling into your gratitude, don't you think? I mean, what would they conclude, seeing your unmentionable just lying discarded with such wanton abandonment?'

'Now that you've had your moment of gloating glory, Mr Jerome, I suggest you cut your losses and go. Before I give that newspaper friend of yours the scoop of the century about the celebrated, sainted Todd Jerome.'

'Was that a threat?'

'No, Mr Jerome. Quite the contrary. But if that's the way you want to take it . . .' Kris shrugged. 'So don't you think you'd better put in an appearance out there before your reporter friend gets suspicious?'

Todd Jerome stood his ground and Kris gave an exaggerated sigh.

'You said yourself that this was just a moment out of time. Well, now we have to get back to and on with our lives, you to the city and your apparent political aspirations, and me, I have to get back to . . .' Kris paused.

Back to what? To her old life? How could she, after this? Would it ever be quite the same again? Somehow she thought not.

'To the country and away from me,' Todd finished softly for her.

'Well,' Kris hesitated and Todd raised one mocking dark brow.

'So go on, Kris. Say it. I have to get away from you.' Her gaze fell beneath the intensity of his.

'There's no way you can honestly say it, is there?' His husky voice rippled over her neatly plaited emotions, and they began to unravel. 'Let's stop playing games, Kris.'

'I don't know what you mean.' Kris tried valiantly to hold her composure together.

'I mean there's unfinished business between us. You and I, Kris Quade; it will never be finished.'

Their eyes held, blazed, tension holding them spellbound for long, emotive moments. Until Kris tore her gaze from his.

'Don't be silly.' She gave some semblance of a laugh. 'There's nothing between us. We're from two totally different backgrounds, worlds apart. This...' Kris indicated the crash site with a slightly unsteady hand, 'This will... It's all just like a dream, a nightmare. But it will fade.'

'Will it? I don't think so, Kris.'

'It will if we let it, if we ensure that it does,' Kris said with far more conviction than she felt. 'And if you're concerned about what I'll tell that reporter when we get back to Townsville then you can stop worrying. I won't be selling my story to the highest bidder.'

'That's such a relief, my dear,' he said with obvious sarcasm. 'Then I take it you're not going to be a kiss and tell either, Mrs Quade?'

'Tell what?' Kris feigned disinterest. 'I have nothing to say about your kisses, Mr Jerome. Except, what kisses? I've already forgotten them.' She rested one hand casually on her hip. 'How could you even suspect otherwise?'

'Forgive me for misunderstanding,' he bit out scornfully, 'but I seem to recall only minutes ago you were threatening... No.' He held up one strong hand. 'My apologies. You were cautioning me with a scoop for our resident newspaper hound, hmm?' His dark brows rose again.

'My *caution*——' Kris emphasised the word '—had nothing to do with reporters or romantic displays. What I meant was that I was about to tear the wing off this aeroplane and beat you about the head with it.'

He blinked at her, and for a moment she thought she had nonplussed him. Then, to her consternation, he burst out laughing. Reaching past her affronted body, he collected his bag and briefcase.

'You are really something, Kris Quade,' he said, shaking his head. 'And as you've made me so aware of pending newspaper scoops, I think I *had* better go, before I remind you very convincingly about those kisses you're so adamant you've forgotten.'

Before she could glean his intention he had planted a quick, hard kiss on her mouth and was gone.

The journey back to Townsville in the helicopter wasn't the most enjoyable flight Kris could remember, but it seemed to be accomplished in no time at all.

And somehow she couldn't seem to get her dulled brain to function. She just couldn't think. She knew she should, that there were lots of things she had to plan. What they would say when they arrived back in Townsville. How she would conceal her attraction to Todd Jerome from everyone, from him.

She simply sat in a dazed stupor, barely aware of the pilot, the sharp-eyed reporter, and of Todd Jerome himself, sitting so close beside her, his broad shoulder warm against hers.

Dressed now in her jeans and short-sleeved shirt, Kris began to feel the shock of their misadventure, and the closer they got to civilisation the more she craved a long, hot bath.

Todd had changed, too, into a pair of grey trousers and a pale blue short-sleeved knit shirt, and he couldn't have looked less like a man who had spent days stranded in the outback.

As they flew over the city and began their descent, Kris gazed out at the activities of the airport they had left just two days earlier. She felt decidedly desensitised now. Light-headed. And when Matt Kane opened the door for her she tumbled out into his arms.

'Whoa! I'll have to get in on these rescues more often. I could get to like beautiful women throwing themselves at me in gratitude,' he remarked humorously and Kris managed to smile as she righted herself. 'Think you can walk across to the terminal?' he asked with concern.

Kris nodded.

'Rats! And I was hoping to make an entrance carrying the fair damsel in her moment of distress.'

'Well, stay close,' Kris advised him with a laugh. 'Who knows what might happen between here and the doorway?'

'I suggest we get going.' Todd Jerome began to stride towards the terminal and Kris heard Matt's soft chuckle as they hurried after him.

They entered the building and pandemonium seemed to break out. Cameras flashed. Voices rose in a confusion of unintelligible questions. Bodies surged forward in a heaving, pulsating mass.

Kris tensed in appalled horror. Her throat went dry and she had trouble drawing a breath, her eyes darting across the sea of seething faces. Her trembling hand rose to fend off the encroaching throng just as the whole scene began to waver and then spin sickeningly before her.

For the very first time in her life Kris sank to the floor in a dead faint.

She didn't hear the sudden cessation of the noise, nor did she see Todd Jerome shoulder everyone out of the way. And she was totally unaware that he had gathered her into his strong arms and forced his way through the crowd to the medical team waiting behind the journalists. Every camera flashed.

CHAPTER SEVEN

KRIS came to in the ambulance and she fought to orientate herself. She felt the motion of the vehicle and for a moment she was back in the Cessna, flying over the dry, dusty outback.

Her eyelids fluttered and a handsome face took form in her line of vision. Dark hair. Grey eyes. Square jaw with a faint cleft in the chin. She blinked again. Who was he?

She opened her mouth and closed it just as quickly as it all fell into place. Todd Jerome. The crash. Their plight—stranded in the outback—and their subsequent rescue.

Her eyes moved around the ambulance and she frowned bewilderedly.

'You're all right, Kris.' Todd's deep voice assaulted her weakened defences. 'You just fainted back at the terminal.'

'Where are we going?' She tried to get her tangled thoughts unjumbled.

'To the hospital. For a check-up.'

'The hospital.' Kris tried to sit up, but Todd's hand on her shoulder made her lie back. 'I don't want to go to the hospital. I want to go home. To Amaroo.' Her lip trembled and she caught it between her teeth.

'Come on, Biggles. We're nearly there. You've shown strength most men would find it hard to match. Don't let me down now.' His resonant voice held that teasing, provoking quality she had come to recognise and she drew a sharp breath.

'A man? Why is it always a man who's looked upon as the gauge against which strength is measured?' she remarked with some of her old fire. 'I'll admit that physically...' She looked up at him and stopped speaking, for his mouth twitched into a smile he couldn't quite conceal. 'You're taking a rise out of me, aren't you?' Kris demanded and he gave her a wounded look.

'Who, me? Would I dare, Biggles?'

'Stop calling me that!' she commanded and he shook his head.

'Tsk! Tsk! Such a virago! You know, I'm just a little surprised you allowed our plane to go down. I mean, I'd have expected you to hold it in the sky by sheer force of will.'

Kris folded her arms and turned away from him, only to glance back at him when he gave a low chuckle.

'It wasn't so funny when we were marooned in the back of beyond,' she reminded him. 'But I guess it's a different story now we're home safely.'

'It wasn't so bad, was it? Out there?' he asked softly, and Kris's nerve-endings began to execute an eager tattoo. 'I have to admit I rather enjoyed it.'

'*You* might have, but I can assure you I didn't care for it at all.' Kris's voice was firm enough, but she couldn't hold his gaze.

'None of it, Biggles?' he queried lightly, his tone impossibly more inciting. 'Not even this——'

'Don't!' Kris held up her hand. 'Please. We agreed we were going to forget—well, forget what happened this morning.'

'I wasn't aware we'd reached a decision on that point. Seems to me we rather left the conclusion hanging a trifle up in the air.'

'Todd, please. If you have any decency at all you'll do as I ask,' Kris appealed to him.

He was silent for long moments. 'And what do you ask, Kris? That we pretend it never happened? That we try to wipe out all memories of the event? That I shake hands with you, thank you sincerely for saving my life, and walk blithely away?'

'You're exaggerating.' Kris swallowed. 'I hardly did any life-saving. And, anyway, you reciprocated with the snake.' She barely repressed a shudder. 'But, forgetting what happened, well——' she swallowed again '—it's not inconceivable, is it?'

'Come on, Kris. What you're suggesting is well nigh impossible.'

'I don't see why.' Kris's heartbeats gave an agitated flutter. How she'd love to read more into his reasons for not wanting to walk away. And yet at the same time she was terrified to even think about it. Involvement with Todd Jerome would be the very height of foolishness. It would be rather like taking a step off solid rock on to extremely shaky ground.

'Don't you?' he asked levelly.

'Oh, good grief. I don't understand why you're making such an issue of it. Unless it was the circumstances that you found so titillating. Our——' Kris paused '—fling can't have been a novelty for the great Todd Jerome. Women probably throw themselves into your bed at a great rate of knots. And I'd hazard a guess you forget them just as quickly. All I'm asking is that you do the same with regard to me. What's so difficult about that?'

'And if I refuse?' He was scrutinising her through narrowed eyes.

'I can't see why you would want to refuse. I shouldn't imagine it would be quite the thing an up-and-coming political candidate would want splashed all over the front page of the Sunday papers.'

'Now that would really be something, wouldn't it? It would make such fascinating reading. And it works both ways, you know. The prim and proper, so very moral widow Quade in such a compromising position. Perhaps your uncle will demand I untarnish the family name and make an honest woman of you,' he countered harshly as the ambulance door swung open.

They had reached the hospital without either of them being aware that the vehicle was no longer in motion.

As they were helped from the ambulance they studiously ignored each other and Kris decided it was most fortunate that they were competently propelled in opposite directions.

Two doctors gave Kris a thorough examination and then she was taken by a friendly young nurse for the exquisite pleasure of a hot bath.

'I can imagine how much you're looking forward to this. Three days out in the heat and dust without running water must have been the pits.'

'It certainly was,' Kris agreed as she tested the temperature of the water. 'I can't wait to soak off all the grime.'

'But at least you did have one consolation,' said the nurse and Kris raised her eyebrows enquiringly. 'You had that gorgeous hunk, Todd Jerome, all to yourself. What a windfall. He's the sexiest man around.'

'Mmmm,' Kris murmured non-committally, concentrating on the water swirling into the bath.

'Can you believe he's going into politics?' continued the nurse. 'What a body! And those come-to-bed eyes! He'd be fantastic in the movies, the next Mel Gibson in no time. Still, if he wants to run the country he's got my vote before he even makes a campaign speech. Talk about charisma. Wow!' She sighed expressively as she left Kris to slide into her bath.

Looks, Kris muttered to herself as she let the water play over her, were very deceiving. Todd Jerome might be as handsome as all get out, but he was still the most arrogant, overbearing, egotistical . . . Her teeth clenched at the long list of his shortcomings.

Come-to-bed eyes, indeed! His rugged face came into focus in her mind's eye and then she remembered the feel of his lips covering hers, the tumult of emotions as his hands had moved assuredly over her body.

The warm water cooled by comparison as her skin grew hot. She shivered as the sensations swept over her and, try as she might, she couldn't seem to banish them from her anguished mind.

Angrily she took the sponge and began to scrub her body in an effort to wipe away any trace of those erotic moments, but even as she rubbed at her skin she knew she was fighting a losing battle. Todd Jerome had left his mark on her and she was sure it would take more than a hot bath to remove him from her perfidious memories.

When the nurse returned she grinned broadly at Kris and held up a clean pair of jeans and a loose sweat-shirt.

'Yours, I believe.' She chuckled as she passed the clothes to Kris, who removed her towel sarong and pulled on the jeans before slipping the shirt over her head. 'There's a young man called Josh out there who assures me it's your very favourite sweat-shirt and that you had to have it immediately.'

'Thanks.' Kris smiled. 'And Josh is right—it is my favourite. So Donna and my uncle are here too?' Kris's voice shook and the nurse patted her arm.

'Yes. All waiting in your room.'

'Room?' Kris blinked. 'But I'm fine. I thought I'd be going home.'

'Such gratitude!' The nurse tut-tutted with mock severity. 'We're keeping you and Mr Jerome here over-night, just for observation.'

'But I'm not sick,' Kris protested.

'Of course you're not.' The nurse's tone was typically soothing. 'Let's call it simple precautions. All you have to do is relax. I promise you, you'll enjoy it.' She opened the door and motioned Kris into the hall. 'Well, not as much as sleeping under the stars with Todd Jerome, but all good things must come to an end.' She laughed aloud at the look on Kris's face.

Kris followed the nurse along a sterile-looking corridor and into what was obviously a private room. The décor was comforting and light, but Kris only noticed that later. Her attention went immediately to the small boy who sat alone on the bed, trainered feet moving back and forth, his face set in a serious frown.

'Josh!' Kris ran over and lifted him into her arms, clasping him to her.

Josh hugged her back, planting wet kisses over her cheek.

'Mum told me you were OK, but I thought she was just saying that. Did the plane get all crunched up?' he asked, his eyes wide.

'Just a little.' Kris sank on to the bed beside him and smoothed back his soft hair. 'But where's your mother and your grandfather?' she enquired as the door opened.

Kris turned as her cousin joined them. Donna was smiling broadly and came forward to hug Kris herself.

'What a relief to have you back in one piece. Dad and I were beginning to think...' She stopped and glanced quickly at Josh. 'What an adventure,' she finished and her fears hung unspoken between them.

Tears welled in Kris's eyes, but she blinked them back. 'I'm glad to be back, too,' she said softly.

'Dad will be here soon,' Donna continued. 'He's talking to the air safety people.'

Kris sighed. 'I guess I'll have to see them as well. Uncle Ted must be upset about the Cessna. I'm afraid it may be a complete write-off.'

'Good grief, Kris! Forget about the silly plane. Dad couldn't care less about it. Planes can be replaced. You can't.'

She sank down into a chair. 'We were pretty worried when they couldn't find you on your flight path,' she added carefully as Josh slid off the bed and went to gaze out of the window. 'But at least you're both home safely.' Donna smiled. 'That's all that matters.'

'And I'm perfectly all right, you know, so I don't really need to stay here tonight,' Kris told her cousin.

'Enjoy it while you can, Kris,' Donna suggested. 'At least in here the reporters won't be able to get to you. They've been chasing us ever since we arrived in Townsville.'

'I don't understand it. It was unbelievable at the airport. They were like a swarm of killer bees.' Kris frowned. 'Why on earth are they so interested? Usually in cases like this, once a missing aircraft's been found there's just a small report in the papers and it's forgotten.'

'Small report!' Donna pulled a face. 'Your crash and the search have been front-page news daily. I told you Todd's been the flavour of the month for literally months.'

'Oh. Yes. That's right. I'd almost forgotten about that.'

'Didn't he tell you about his political aspirations?' Donna asked in surprise, and Kris shook her head.

'No. Actually he didn't.' Kris kept her voice as detached as she could. 'We didn't really discuss it.' Todd Jerome had been far too busy baiting her, she wanted to add.

'For heaven's sake, what on earth did you talk about, then?'

Kris shrugged. 'I don't know. Nothing much. Inconsequential stuff mostly, I think.' She glanced at Donna's raised eyebrows. 'It all seems rather unreal now,' she finished lamely.

'And talking about unreal, that about describes him, doesn't it?' Donna beamed. 'I have to admit it did cross my mind that you'd fallen for him and decided to spirit him away.'

'Donna!' Kris remonstrated and her cousin laughed.

'Just joking. But I sure wish I'd been there to see your face when you first met him. Go on, Kris. Admit you found him stop-you-in-your-tracks attractive.'

'I suppose he is nice enough looking,' Kris began, and Donna gave an exclamation of disbelief.

'My God, Kris! There are millions of women who are going to be dead green with envy. They'd give their eye-teeth to have been trapped out there with Todd Jerome.'

'I'm sorry to shatter the romantic ideal, Donna, but it wasn't all that much fun.'

'I don't believe it.' Donna pulled an ambivalent face and folded her arms. 'Perhaps you need a week in hospital to have your head read. I could give you a list of women who, if they were given the choice of being stranded with Todd Jerome or Tom Cruise, would pick Todd without needing a moment to consider.'

Kris could only shrug and hope her face showed no inkling of the direction of her wayward thoughts. This wasn't the time to remember how foolish she'd been over Todd Jerome.

But Donna seemed to be too involved in her own musings about her idea of God's gift to women.

'If I didn't adore Rob so much I'd give you a run for your money where Todd Jerome's concerned,' she said airily. 'However, now that I've seen you're undamaged by your ordeal, what about Todd Jerome? Someone said something about his leg. Should I go and pay my respects to the man in question?' She winked at Kris. 'It's the least I can do, I suppose. After all, it was sort of my fault, wasn't it? I mean, he was on his way out to Amaroo at my invitation so I guess you could say I was responsible for putting him in the wrong place at the wrong time, and apparently——' Donna grimaced at Kris '—with the wrong woman.'

With a meaningful look at her cousin she stood up and walked jauntily out of the room, telling Josh to stay with Kris until his grandfather joined them.

And, although Kris listened to Donna's son's lively chatter, part of her attention wandered, kept going back to Todd Jerome, leaving her with a whole lot of thoughts she refused to allow herself to dwell on, not the least of them being a surge of something she suspected was rather akin to regret.

It was some time before Kris could get to sleep that night. The hospital bed seemed far too soft, the air-conditioned atmosphere too cloying, the sounds of civilisation suddenly absurdly loud, and her mind was far too active. Her thoughts ran around in circles like a joy ride at a carnival, and about as colourfully.

Eventually she took herself to task. Life was going to go on just as it had before the crash. Before she met Todd Jerome. She would go back to Amaroo with Uncle Ted, Donna and Josh and she'd pick up her life where she'd left off less than a week ago.

And forget she'd fallen for the so obvious charms of a good-looking Lothario. Everyone was entitled to one indiscretion, she rationalised irritably.

Yet how on earth was she going to forget? she taunted herself unmercifully. Making love with Todd Jerome had been the most exciting, most electrifying experience in her life. And no matter how hard she tried to relegate the incident to the darkest, furthest reaches of her mind, she knew she would never be able to banish that mistake from her consciousness.

And as she lay in the cocoon of her hospital room, yearning for the sanctuary of Amaroo and normality, those moments kept playing over and over again like the steamy sequence from a low-grade movie. She had every movement, every nuance printed indelibly behind her eyes. Was it any wonder, she asked herself, that she continued to toss restlessly for what seemed like hours?

But she must have fallen asleep at some stage for she was woken far too soon by the cheery entry of a nurse with her breakfast. Desultorily, she pushed the food around her plate until she decided she wasn't going to stay languishing in bed a moment longer. Carefully she pushed away her almost untouched breakfast tray and threw back the covers. Her clothes had to be somewhere. Once showered and dressed, she knew she'd feel so much better. She swung her feet over the side of the high bed just as someone tapped on her door and before she had her bare feet on the floor the door opened.

For one wildly quixotic split second she dared hope——

'Good morning. And how's my favourite heroine?' Matt Kane beamed as he softly closed the door behind him.

Kris sank on to the bed, for her knees had gone suddenly weak. And she knew it had nothing to do with the sudden appearance of the reporter.

'Over your exploits?' He crossed the room, his eyes moving appreciatively over Kris's body, and she folded her arms in unconscious self-defence.

'Yes, and I'm looking forward to going home. In fact I was about to get dressed,' she added pointedly, but her undisguised hint fell on deaf ears.

'So what was it like stranded out there?' he asked, sitting down beside her on the hospital bed.

Kris moved slightly, putting a millimetre more space between them. 'Pretty scary, as you can imagine,' she replied carefully. 'Logically, I told myself we'd be found as soon as the search area was widened. However, when you find yourself in that kind of situation you don't always think rationally.'

Or act rationally, Kris reminded herself and then wished she hadn't as her face grew hot.

'Did you ever lose hope you'd be found?' Matt asked softly and Kris relaxed a little.

'When we sighted the aircraft and it flew off, I'd say that was the lowest point for me.' She sighed and glanced at the man beside her. 'But we were found, so...' She shrugged eloquently.

'OK. Let's get to the good bits. What was it like being marooned with a celebrity like Todd Jerome?' Matt's eyes danced mischievously and Kris decided his easy manner must be his best asset in his business.

'Am I to take that as an interested enquiry or a leading question?' she asked drily and Matt grinned.

'Very sharp, Kris. A bit of both, I guess. So does that mean your lips are sealed?'

'It was no big deal. Better than being stranded alone,' she replied carefully and he laughed.

'The next thing you'll be confiding is that Todd used the time to go over some of the paperwork he just happened to have with him.'

Kris could almost wish he had.

'Although,' Matt continued, 'knowing Todd I can imagine he was a trifle frustrated at not being able to get back to his desk and his clients. I'm always telling him he's a workaholic. So, did he give you a bad time?'

'No. No, not really. Why would you think that?' Kris glanced casually at her fingernails.

'Ahhh.' Matt drew out the soft exclamation and Kris turned to look at him again, her eyebrows rising questioningly.

'"Ahhh" what?' she asked him levelly and he laughed softly.

'Ahhh, didn't you find Todd Jerome irresistible?'

'Should I have?' Kris asked disdainfully, playing for time and the opportunity to change the direction of the conversation.

Matt's mouth twitched in amusement. 'Not at all. I was just going on past personal observations on the subject. It may surprise you to know that the whole marriageable female population went into mourning while Todd was missing. It was unbelievable. I helped out where I could but——' he shrugged exaggeratedly '—it was a tough job.'

'I can well imagine.' A reluctant smile lifted the corners of Kris's mouth.

'That's better.' Matt took her hand, holding it in one of his. 'I was beginning to think you were as uptight as Todd seems to be these days. But I knew you were far too intelligent and discerning to throw yourself away on Todd. Especially when there's someone much more appealing to a gorgeous-looking woman like yourself and with a more manageable public profile awaiting you in the wings.'

'And does this appealing, more manageable profile have a name?' Kris asked with a smile.

'But of course. Me.' Matt beamed. 'Who else?'

'Now how do I answer that?' Kris spoke as lightly as she could. 'You being so appealing, et cetera, you must have your own——' she paused '—following. And I've already evoked the wrath of the marriageable female population once. Dare I do it again?'

'Live dangerously. That's my motto,' he suggested softly, looking deeply into Kris's still amused eyes.

Before Kris could form an equally wittily outrageous reply, for the second time that morning there was a light tap on her door and the door swung open.

This morning he wore jeans and a loose white sweat-
shirt, the long sleeves pushed casually halfway to his
elbows. He must have just showered for his hair was
darkly damp, curling slightly at the back, and she noticed
a small mark on his jawline where he appeared to have
cut himself shaving.

Kris could only gaze at him, unable to move, her eyes
drinking in the solid masculine symmetry of him, and
all her previously resolved good intentions flew out the
window without so much as a scruple. So much for
putting it all behind her.

She blinked as if in shock. He was impossibly more
handsome this morning than her recalcitrant thoughts
of the evening before had invoked. His well worn blue
jeans hugged his narrow hips and muscular thighs and
Kris had to steel herself against an almost overwhelming
urge to allow her eyes to slide slowly, savouringly over
him.

What would he do if she gave in to the impulse to
throw discretion to the wind and fall into his strong arms,
lose her fingers in his thick dark hair, mould her mouth
to his?

His eyes did a quick survey of the scene before him,
took in Matt and Kris sitting side by side on her bed,
and settled on Kris's hand still clasped firmly in Matt's.

Guiltily Kris made to snatch her hand away, but Matt
held her fingers fast for long seconds before slowly,
almost casually releasing her.

'Todd! You look none the worse for wear this
morning,' Matt remarked pleasantly as he lounged easily
on Kris's bed.

Todd's eyes had narrowed and Kris could see the tense
set of his jaw. 'I'm fine,' he replied levelly enough. 'Does
Kris's doctor know you're here pestering her, Matt? Or
didn't you know we'd put a total ban on the Press?'

'Press!' Matt put a hand theatrically to his heart. 'I thought I was more friend than Press. Can't I just enquire after Kris's health? And yours, of course, old friend,' he added with a grin.

'No interviews at this time, Matt,' Todd said lightly and Kris sensed tension in the man beside her now, too.

'OK.' He sighed exaggeratedly. 'I guess that means it's time to take my leave.' He turned to Kris and before she knew his intention he had bent over to kiss her lightly on the cheek. 'Look after yourself, Kris. I'll be seeing you.'

With that he winked audaciously at her and left her with Todd Jerome.

Todd closed the door which Matt had left ajar behind him and leant easily back against it. 'How are you?' he asked quietly, his voice low, and Kris took a shallow breath, exhilarated and yet just a little anxious now that she was alone with him.

Did he know just how seductive his mellow tone sounded in the muffled quietness of the hospital room? 'I'm all right.' Her own voice came out slightly husky and she shrugged. 'And you?'

'No problems.' He flexed his shoulders. 'Couldn't seem to get used to the bed though.'

'I had the same trouble.' Kris swallowed, flushing as his grey eyes slid over the folds of her oversized nightshirt. How she wished it was as long as it was wide, for it barely reached her knees. She crossed her arms protectively over her breasts and tried valiantly to appear as relaxed as he was. 'What did the doctor say about your leg?'

'Nothing to worry about. It's all stitched up and should heal nicely,' he said almost absently and shoved his hands into the pockets of his jeans. 'How long had Matt Kane been here?'

His words dragged Kris's gaze from the taut material moulding his strong thighs. 'Not long,' she got out over her dry lips.

'You seemed to be getting along fairly well. In fact, you looked pretty——' he paused '—cosy.'

Kris's chin rose as his meaning dawned. 'Cosy?' she repeated sharply.

He inclined his head, pushing himself upright, away from the door, taking a couple of steps into the room, closer to Kris, and she felt every muscle, every sinew in her body flex tautly, waiting.

'Quite the confidant, is Matt Kane.' His tone was even and his eyes had narrowed again, shielding his thoughts. 'As many people have learned to their cost.'

Kris raised her eyebrows.

'A casual word in conversation can become front-page news.'

'That's not a very flattering insinuation,' she said levelly. 'I thought you were friends.'

He gave a soft laugh. 'More acquaintances.'

'Well, rest assured I'm not quite as gullible as you seem to think I am.'

'Don't trust him, Kris. Not when there's a hot story in the offing. Making news makes his living and he'll do anything to get his story.'

Kris flushed. If he meant Matt would resort to flirting to get his scoop then she was well aware of that. 'I'm sure you're exaggerating,' Kris began as she moistened her still dry lips with her tongue-tip.

'I'm not, you know.'

'I see no reason for anyone to hound me for a story. It's all over, surely? We've been found and rescued, with no gruesome injuries to report. It's old hat now.'

He strode forward and Kris's nerve-endings tensed on full alert. 'Take a look out of the window.'

Kris walked around the bed as he held back the curtains. She drew back at the sight of the two news vans, their crews standing around talking.

'Matt Kane is part of that and somehow he got past the security here.' His soft tone played over her nerve-endings and she moved to disguise the slight shiver that tingled over her.

'You'd be advised to stay away from him,' he added imperiously, his intonation now implying much more to the meaning of his words, and Kris stiffened.

Why was he really warning her against Matt Kane? Because he knew she was an easy target for a practised philanderer?

Mortified, Kris drew herself together. Still, he had no right to tell her what she should or shouldn't do. 'I take your point about guarding my tongue,' she said succinctly, 'but I'm sure Matt wouldn't use anything we discussed this morning.'

'No?' He raised a mocking dark brow.

'No!' Kris repeated with more conviction than she felt. She suspected Matt Kane was astute enough to be busily reading between the lines of what she'd said, but she wasn't going to tell Todd Jerome that.

'I'd still prefer it if you kept away from him.'

'And if I don't?' Kris challenged dulcetly, her eyes meeting and holding his in a battle of wills.

The ensuing silence that met her provocative words stretched into a charged, uncomfortable stillness that seemed to echo between them, and the heightened tension rose to an almost incendiary level.

What would have resulted they would never know, for at that moment the door was pushed open and young Josh raced into the room. His step faltered a little when he noticed the tall man beside Kris, but he continued on to throw himself against her.

'I'm glad I didn't dream you up last night,' he said as he kissed her cheek, and Kris hugged him.

'What are you doing on your own?'

'Mum and Uncle Ted are talking to the doctor about when you can leave the hospital,' Josh told her as he gazed solemnly at Todd Jerome. 'Is he a doctor, too?' he whispered loudly.

'No. This is Mr Jerome. He was in the plane with me when we had to crash-land,' Kris told him. 'Mr Jerome, this is Donna's son, Josh Bradman.'

Josh stood facing Todd, eyes summing up the tall man, before he formally extended his hand. 'How do you do, Mr Jerome? Thank you for looking after Kris when the plane crashed.'

Todd took the small outstretched hand with equal gravity. 'It was my pleasure.' His eyes rose to meet Kris's, his expression adding far more meaning to the words, and she felt a stab of purely physical desire course through her.

Her heartbeats clamoured in her breast and she only just quelled the urge to press her hand to her heart. She had to keep her composure, stop herself revealing her feelings to this man, betraying herself and her attraction to him.

'Guess what? I'm going for a ride in your rescue helicopter later,' Josh was saying excitedly. 'It'll be great.' He turned to Kris. 'Maybe you can come and watch before you leave for Brisbane.'

'Brisbane?' Kris frowned. 'Josh, what on earth are you talking about?'

'Mum says you'll need a holiday after your ord...ord-something,' Josh explained. 'So she told Uncle Ted you should have a few weeks in Brisbane.' He frowned. 'Don't you want to go?'

'Well, we'll see.' Kris floundered, not looking at Todd. 'I'll have to talk to your mother.'

'About what?' Kris's cousin breezed into the room like a breath of fresh air. 'Hello again, Todd. You look all recovered this morning. No after-effects from your experience?' She smiled at Todd and put one small hand on his arm.

Todd smiled easily, his hand covering Donna's. 'No. Or at least none that I can't handle,' he said, his gaze meeting and holding Kris's, and she felt her colour rise. 'In retrospect we wouldn't have missed it for the world, would we, Kris?'

'I'm sure you're joking, Mr Jerome,' she replied shortly and turned to Donna. 'Did the doctor say when I can leave the hospital?' she asked and Donna raised her eyebrows.

'He's on his way to give you a final check-over. Anyone would think you didn't like this place.'

'I'd just like to get home to Amaroo.' Kris sighed. 'And put all this behind me,' she added without meeting Todd's gaze.

'That's understandable,' Donna agreed easily. 'It must have been awful for both of you.'

Kris looked quickly at her cousin, but Donna was keeping her expression bland.

'But as to going straight back to Amaroo,' Donna continued, 'that's what the doctor wants to talk to you about. He agreed with me that you should have a bit of a break, give yourself time to get over the shock. You've been through quite an ordeal, you know.'

'Yes, an ordeal,' Josh piped up. 'That was it. You need a holiday after an ordeal, Kris.' He grinned at her. 'We were pretty worried about you, you know. But you'll be fine after Mr Jerome takes you down to Brisbane with him.'

CHAPTER EIGHT

KRIS stood up and crossed to the open sliding glass doors that led on to the balcony of Todd's unit high above the snaking Brisbane River. It was a large apartment in a prestigious block on the south bank of the river, looking across its reaches to the freeway and high-rise buildings of the city, brightly lit against the night sky.

Stepping outside into the cooling breeze, she rested her arms on the railings and gazed across at the city, not really seeing it.

The view, Kris knew already, was quite spectacular, and someone had done a fantastic job with the interior decoration of the spacious three-bedroom apartment.

Thick-pile beige carpet cushioned the floor and the dark lounge where Kris had been sitting smelled of polished wood and genuine leather. Off to the left, behind a light Chinese screen, was a compact kitchen and a breakfast bar with high stools. The formal dining-room was set apart from the living-room and the bedrooms were to the right.

What had possessed her to allow herself to be talked into accompanying Todd Jerome down to Brisbane? she asked herself for the umpteenth time. She should have gone back to Amaroo. There had been nothing physically wrong with her and all the palaver about rest and recuperation and delayed shock seemed pretty ridiculous.

So she'd fainted at the airport terminal, but anyone would have felt disoriented with all those noisy reporters crowding in on them. She had never considered herself to be spineless or even remotely cowardly.

112

Yet she'd capitulated with nary a struggle when Todd had turned on his undeniable charm. He had that effect on her. And the fact frightened her.

'Dad and I thought you deserved a break, a holiday,' Donna had said as she stood in Kris's hospital room, her glance going swiftly from Kris to Todd, sensing the tightness of the atmosphere between them.

'We've both been through a pretty traumatic time, Kris,' Todd put in evenly as he stepped forward. 'And, although we have no serious physical injuries, the doctors suggested we both take it easy for a few weeks. Your uncle and I decided my place in Brisbane would be ideal.'

'I can't just up sticks and jaunt down to Brisbane with you,' Kris stated. 'I have responsibilities——'

'You don't have to worry about Amaroo,' Donna added quickly. 'Dad's already arranged for someone to help out temporarily.'

Kris raised her eyebrows.

'We don't mean we don't want you to come home, Kris,' Donna assured her, 'but... well, Amaroo is so isolated and you've had a pretty big shock and everything. Besides, you don't have to bury yourself in the back of beyond.'

'I don't consider that's what I'd be doing,' Kris said tersely, feeling as though the control of her life was being taken out of her hands.

'Well, I'll leave you two to discuss it.' Donna took hold of her son's hand. 'Josh and I will go and find my father.'

'I simply suggested my place as an alternative to a motel or a rented unit, mainly because of the security it provides from the reporters who will try to bug you,' Todd said placatingly as the door closed behind Donna and her son, and Kris's anger bristled.

'Meaning Matt Kane, I take it?' Kris exclaimed.

'Including Matt Kane,' he said levelly.

'I don't understand this.' Kris raised her hands and let them fall. 'If it's seclusion from prying reporters that's paramount then surely Amaroo would be perfect?'

'From a medical point of view the city would be more prudent,' he put in, and Kris took a deep breath.

'I am not sick,' she enunciated emphatically.

'Maybe not at the moment, but shock can affect people in different ways. What if you should suffer from the symptoms of delayed reaction in a day or two? You owe it to yourself to be closer to medical help than an out-lying cattle station.'

Kris ran an agitated hand through her fair hair. 'Why do I feel as if I'm being manipulated?' she asked with a little less belligerence.

'Besides, I owe you, Kris.' His voice was softly sincere.

'Owe me? What could you possibly owe me?' Kris challenged.

'You did land the plane safely. My leg.' He shrugged affably.

Kris expelled a breath in exasperation. 'So I had to make a forced landing. But once we were on the ground you were never in any danger, and you know it.'

'Debatable, Kris.'

'I told you before that you returned the favour by re-moving that snake. And I'm not coming to Brisbane with you,' she stated with conviction. 'It...it wouldn't be...it wouldn't be right.'

'Let me guess. Right, as in morally correct?' He leant casually back against the end of the bed, strong arms folded across his chest.

'I'm not in the habit of cohabiting with men.' Kris felt the heat of colour tint her face. 'If that makes me old-fashioned and somewhat *passée* then so be it. I can live with that, believe me.'

'Habits can be broken.'

'Only when the addicted want them to be.'

'Or when they're marooned in the outback awaiting rescue.' His deep voice confronted, accosted her senses, and Kris swung away from him as her anger turned on herself.

'I won't discuss that,' she said flatly and she felt him move, step closer to her.

Steeling herself, she faced him again.

'You have my word it will all be terribly above-board,' he told her, and Kris raised her eyebrows sceptically. 'My mother will be there to chaperon us.'

'Your mother?' Kris repeated in surprise and then gave him a dubious look.

'On my honour.' He placed his hand in the region of his heart. 'My mother's agreed to come and stay for the duration and she's nearly beside herself with pleasure at the assignment. She can't wait to meet you.'

Kris's resolve showed signs of weakening and she valiantly sought to repair the damage. 'You're simply using that to manipulate me. Don't think I don't know that.' But her words lacked the necessary conviction in her ears. To even contemplate going anywhere with this man was the height of foolishness. So why was she considering it?

'I wouldn't call it manipulation exactly, but I admit I don't want to lose touch with you.'

He gave her a derisive smile, which she suspected was aimed more at himself, and she gazed up at him, into the grey depths of his eyes. A tingle of awareness came to life in the pit of her stomach, spread upwards, flared to engulf her entire body.

'I don't...' She swallowed convulsively. 'I don't know what you're talking about.'

'Of course you do,' he told her silkily. 'We strike sparks off each other, Kris. Why don't we enjoy the fire?'

'We don't...we haven't even known each other for a week,' she said through lips that were loath to form the

words. Yet how she wanted to take hold of the ball he
was tossing her, and run with the exhilaration of it.

'Four days, to be precise. A second or a century, Kris—
what does it matter? But I do know this: I don't want
to lose you from my life.'

He stepped closer, and Kris knew he was going to take
her in his arms, kiss her, as he had before... And she
knew she wasn't going to stop him.

In fact she felt herself lean towards him just as a knock
sounded on the door and Donna tentatively stuck her
head into the room.

She took in the scene before her, Kris's instinctive move
to put space between herself and Todd Jerome, and she
grinned broadly. 'Dad's booked a table for lunch for us
all. As soon as you've seen the doctor, changed and
checked out we can go.'

And three days later she was just as unsure of Todd's
intentions; that was the biggest problem. She knew he
wanted her physically. She couldn't deny she wanted him
too. But that could never be enough for her. She needed
commitment and, to her, that meant marriage.

She glanced at her wristwatch. Seven forty-five. Todd
had left to drive his mother to her weekly bingo game
and he was going to call on a client on his way back. So
he probably wouldn't return for at least a couple of
hours.

Now she wished she had gone with Mrs Jerome. She'd
asked Kris to go. Here, alone in the silence of the unit,
it was all too easy to brood, to think about things she'd
tried so hard to forget.

Todd Jerome. They had spent the past three days
together, during which Kris had become more and more
on edge, yet the presence of his mother precluded that
they say or do what Todd's eyes told Kris he wanted to

do. And she swung like a pendulum between relief and regret.

If he wanted an affair he'd chosen the wrong woman. As much as she was attracted to him she didn't intend to allow him to use her and then discard her when he found another playmate.

So do something about the disturbing predicament, she told herself forcefully. Tell him. Leave him in no doubt about how she felt. Remind him they had disliked each other on sight. And their brief interlude had simply been 'a moment out of time'. Those were, after all, his words.

Yet...'You were pretty wonderful'. His words came back unbidden and she went absolutely hot all over.

While they were marooned in the outback the sexual tension between them had simmered, and then exploded, to be dispersed in their passionate coming together. He had made that provocative comment in the heady afterglow of their desire. And it shouldn't be held against him, she mockingly reminded herself. Not in the cold, hard light of reality.

Kris straightened, shoving her hands into the pockets of her jeans. If she continued to agonise over it all she'd end up with a king-sized headache.

Perhaps she'd watch a little television. At least that would take her mind off any soul-searching. She re-entered the living-room and was crossing to the wall unit which held the TV set and the stereo when the doorbell pealed. Kris stood stock-still.

Who could it be? One of the many reporters Todd had thus far kept at bay?

No one had buzzed the external intercom so it had to be someone in the building, a neighbour. The block of units had very strict security measures and visitors had to be let into the apartment block by a tenant.

She crossed to the door and put her eye to the security peep-hole. And her heart began to race. Why was he ringing the doorbell?

She had a panic-filled urge to tiptoe quietly away, pretend she wasn't there. But he knew she was. Slowly she unlatched the door and swung it open and her eyes met those of the man filling the doorway.

'Mum forgot her key so I gave her mine. May I come in?' he asked with mock formality.

No! All Kris's defences screamed out against allowing him entry, but her traitorous body overrode her instincts to take the initiative, stepping back, holding open the door. After all, it was his apartment.

He moved forward, passed her, and stood silently waiting.

Kris struggled to pull herself together, made herself close the door after him, walk into the living-room. Her legs were trembling so much that she sank on to the nearest chair.

This was the first time they had been alone together since that emotive moment in Townsville and she watched him cross to lower his long body into the chair opposite her.

'You're...I thought you said you...' Kris took a quick breath. 'I mean, I wasn't expecting you back so early.'

'My client wasn't home. I should have called.' He shrugged.

Was there a slight touch of irony in his tone? Her gaze slid across the carpet to his feet, moved upwards over his denim-clad legs, narrow hips, firm, flat midriff...

She started as he crossed one long leg over the other, causing the leather chair to creak refinedly, and her eyes flashed to his face. He was regarding her with that same shrewd-eyed calculation. Had he planned this? Of course he had, she told herself harshly.

'How did you get into the building?' Kris asked sharply, babbling the first thing that came into her mind. Residents needed their keys for the main entry as well as their units.

'Someone was just leaving and kindly held the door for me.'

'I see.' Kris frowned. A female tenant, no doubt, she reflected disgustedly, her lips pursing, one who should have had more sense than to disregard the rules.

'I must have looked harmless and utterly trustworthy,' he said easily, and Kris raised her eyebrows. 'Does that mean you disagree?' he asked her guilelessly, relaxing against the back of his chair, his arms lightly folded.

Kris shrugged. 'What do you think? But I'd presume this so considerate door-person was not a man.'

'Very perceptive, Biggles. Another compliment on my special charm, hmm?'

Kris felt warm colour wash her cheeks. 'I didn't intend it to be,' she said levelly, resolving not to give him an inch of ground, conversationally or otherwise.

'I'm sure you didn't.' He shifted his position slightly, as though needing to ease tensed muscles. His elbows now rested on the arms of the chair, hands together forming a steeple with his long, sensitive fingers. 'So. Here we are. Alone at last.'

Kris held his dark gaze with no little difficulty, wishing her heartbeats would stop racing, that her nerve-endings would give up their wild tattoo. She tried intrepidly to prevent herself from watching him, or at least to regard him with a certain amount of detachment. To no avail.

Her eyes drank in the firm contours of his jawline, the slight creases that faintly indented his cheeks, the suggestion of a cleft in his firm chin, the strong, sensual curve of his mouth. And he was enjoying her discomfort.

'Todd, I...' She swallowed again. 'I think we should talk.'

He raised one dark brow. 'Talking wasn't exactly what I had in mind. However, what do you want to discuss?' he asked, barely attempting to hide the amusement in his eyes.

Kris's lips tightened. So it was a joke to him. He thought he had her right where he wanted her. Well, she was about to heartily dent his massive ego.

'I'd like to discuss our——' she paused '—relationship, for want of a better word. I feel I should correct any misconceptions you may be harbouring.'

His eyelashes shielded his expression. 'What makes you think I'm harbouring any misconceptions?' he asked reasonably, and Kris bit off an angry exclamation.

'You're being deliberately obtuse.'

'Then why not put it into words of one syllable for me?' he said derisively.

'All right. I think we should sort out this situation because you've been strutting around like a caveman dragging his woman off by the hair ever since we arrived in Brisbane.'

He gazed at her in mock horror. 'Caveman? I'm wounded, Kris. And I wouldn't hurt a hair on your beautiful head.'

He chuckled deeply and Kris pushed herself to her feet as the resonant sound played over her, weakening her resolve.

'I knew this would be impossible. I should never have allowed myself to be railroaded into coming down here with you. It only served to let you be misled into thinking I was...that I had...that we...'

Kris's voice died as he stood to face her, his grey eyes serious now, holding hers.

'That we are so physically attracted to each other that we've spent the past three days creating so much combustion in this place that it's about ready to explode. And there's nothing misleading about that,' he finished bitingly.

'You're being crude,' Kris said thickly. 'And will you please stop talking about... about that.'

'About what?' he asked innocently, infuriatingly.

'About sex,' she spat out. 'That's all it was between us. Heightened tension resulting from a dangerous situation. That equalled pure unadulterated sex.'

'Don't knock it, Kris. Some people never experience what we——'

'Most people wouldn't want to.'

'You make it sound as if we were a couple of animals on heat.'

'I couldn't have described it better myself,' she said contemptuously, and he took a step towards her.

'For heaven's sake, Kris. You want honesty,' he snarled scornfully, 'then try facing the truth yourself.'

'I am being honest,' she denied. 'I always am honest. And you don't like it.'

He ran a hand through his thick dark hair and prowled across the carpet to stand framed in the patio doorway overlooking the cityscape, his hard back towards her.

Kris remained where she was. She knew she couldn't have commanded her weak muscles to move her feet. In fact she was sure of it, as sure as she was that Todd's eyes were taking in none of the attractive city tableau.

Just as suddenly he swung around to face her and she watched him warily, her heartbeats pounding inside her like drum rolls.

'I've never met a woman who could so easily delude herself. Take a look at yourself, Kris. Adult? Honest? Right from the beginning you were quite prepared to lie to me by omission.'

'What do you mean?'

'How about letting me think you were still married when you weren't? Although I suppose you had a justifiable reason why you felt you had to deceive me, Mrs Quade,' he said derisively. 'About Mr Quade.'

Kris caught her breath at the directness of his attack.

'I didn't intend to lie to you,' she acknowledged. 'I just didn't see any purpose in...' She paused, searching for the right words to explain without completely giving herself away. 'I didn't think there was a right time to fit it into our conversation when we were out there, that's all.'

'A right time!' He reiterated the words with a quiet savagery, with barely a movement of his mouth. 'How about just before you fell into my arms?'

'You're disgusting,' Kris bit out furiously, anger now replacing her apprehension.

'Another flattering adjective, hmm?' he taunted with equal fury. 'But let's not get side-tracked from the point under discussion. Aside from the fact that I already knew you were a widow, didn't you think I'd find out eventually?'

'I couldn't see that it was any of your damn business.'

'Hogwash, Kris! You knew I wanted you. And you used your supposed marriage to hold me off.'

Kris's gaze locked with his, but she knew she couldn't deny his accusation. 'I shouldn't have needed to hold you off,' she stated, her chin high, and Todd swore under his breath, his eyes dark with an anger held mightily in check.

'For God's sake, Kris! Get your head out of the sand. You can't live in a vacuum forever. Life goes on. And that includes yours. Your husband is dead and I'm sorry about that, but no one would expect you to throw yourself into the grave after him. You are alive. You could try to start acting as though you are.'

His words sank into her consciousness, yet she felt no pain at their harshness. Hadn't Donna said much the same thing, only far more gently? Still, she couldn't allow him to make light of her feelings for Kel.

'How dare you?' Kris drew a steadying breath and took a step towards him, facing him boldly. 'If you remember, Mr Jerome,' she said through clenched teeth, 'and, allowing that your memory seems somewhat selective, we had only just met.'

She refused to allow him to interrupt. 'I don't suppose it crossed that self-centred little mind of yours that I just might still find it painful to talk about my husband's death to a virtual stranger, to try to explain about being so close to someone that when they've gone you feel you've lost not only them but part of yourself as well.' Kris drew a shaky breath and turned slightly away from him as she fought for control.

He was silent for long moments and then she heard him sigh. 'How long has it been?' he asked flatly, and Kris shook her head slightly, her anger draining away, leaving her simply tired.

'Four years. He had a fall from his horse. It had happened...' she swallowed. 'He'd been thrown half a dozen times before and walked away. But that last time he hit his head on a rock. He died instantly.'

Kris ran a hand tiredly through her hair. 'It was so sudden,' she added, almost to herself. 'That was the part that was so shocking, so unbelievable. One day he was there. And then he was gone.'

'I'm sorry.'

She wasn't even sure she'd heard him voice the words and she turned back to glance at him, blinking to bring him and the present into a focus of sorts. 'He was...' She paused, frowning slightly. 'There's really not much I could say that would do Kel justice. He was simply a nice person.'

When Todd made no comment she looked up at him, steeling herself for one of his cutting remarks. However, he merely watched her, his eyelashes shielding his expression.

She folded her arms, hands subconsciously rubbing her elbows. 'Look, would you like a cup of tea or coffee?'

'Coffee, please,' he said and Kris walked behind the screen in to the kitchenette.

It was more than a relief to be able to do something, to concentrate on going through the motions of measuring out the drip filter-coffee grains, adding the water, and setting out chunky pottery mugs.

He had followed her into the kitchen and was now propped up on a stool behind the breakfast bar. The tension between them had defused somewhat and Kris felt more than a little relieved as they waited in silence, the aroma of the brewing coffee filling the air.

She set his cup on the counter-top in front of him before taking a sip of her own coffee and leaning back against the cupboard opposite him. He stood up immediately and lifted a stool around the bar for her to sit on.

'Thank you. We could go back into the living-room if you like.'

He shook his head. 'This is fine.'

They drank their coffee in silence, each seemingly lost in their own thoughts. Todd's weren't giving him any joy if his expression was any indication. Kris, meanwhile, was suffering her own uncomfortable pangs of what she could only recognise as guilt.

She had loved Kel, she told herself. She'd loved him since she was a child. What she felt for the man sitting opposite her was simply a physical attraction. He was, after all, the most arresting, most magnetic man she had ever met. It was only natural that she would be tempted.

Oh, she'd been tempted all right, she agreed self-derisively. And she had given in to that enticement with scarcely an attempt at resistance. She gazed morosely into the dregs of her coffee. If he touched her now she knew she wouldn't have the power to reject him. So what sort of woman did that make her?

'Kris?'

The sound of her name spoken in his deep seductive tone had her tensing again, all senses suddenly alert, watchful, waiting. Warily she looked up at him and the air between them instantaneously ignited.

Slowly he replaced his coffee-cup on the counter and slid off his stool to move around into the kitchen, his eyes not leaving hers. Deliberately he propelled her into his arms and she could only melt against the solid wall of his chest.

'What the hell have we been doing to each other?' he murmured and his lips found hers.

Kris made a feeble token murmur of protest before her bones seemed to liquefy and she dissolved against him, her breasts soft against the hard wall of his chest, her thighs fusing with his.

They clung tightly together and Todd groaned softly, a deeply erotic sound that vibrated through Kris to the very tips of her fingers and her toes.

When he surrendered her lips they were both breathing raggedly as they fought to catch their breaths.

'Kris Quade, what you do to me,' he murmured hoarsely, his forehead resting lightly against hers, his words playing tantalisingly over her soft, now pliant mouth.

Her lips had to touch his again or she would die. She moved towards him so that she could place quick, soft tiny kisses on the corners of his mouth, moving milli-metres each time until he could bear it no longer and he crushed her to him again.

His lips slid along the line of her jaw, nibbled on the sensitive lobe of her ear, sending shivers of erotic sensations coursing through her. His teeth, his tongue-tip teased the soft skin of her neck to settle at the base of her throat, where her pulse raced in erratic excitement.

Somehow one of his legs had insinuated itself between hers as he forced her back against the counter-top.

'I think perhaps,' he suggested softly, thickly, 'we'd best return to the living-room after all, before we both sink inappropriately to the floor, hmm? That's if your knees are as weak as mine are,' he added self-contemptuously.

Kris gave a soft, throaty chuckle. 'Gone to water,' she agreed and, with their arms entwined, eyes locked together, they found their way from the kitchen to the living-room to sink as one on to the plush leather sofa.

Todd took her hand in his, lifted it to his mouth, his lips slowly, sensuously taking each fingertip into his mouth, his tongue causing slivers of molten desire to erupt in the pit of her stomach.

His mouth teased the soft flesh of the inside of her elbow, nibbled upwards, over the short sleeve of her shirt, to the V of flushed skin exposed in the front.

His fingers expertly dealt with each small button and he pushed aside the material to slide his lips over the mound of her breast.

'You taste divine,' he said thickly, his mouth resting between her breasts above the low lacy line of her bra, 'and I want to savour every wonderful inch of you.'

He unclasped the front clip of her bra and her breasts broke free. For long moments he gazed at her and then he lowered his head to nuzzle each rosy peak in turn.

Kris closed her eyes, let his words, his touch, the pure sensation wash over her, and her trembling hands unsteadily helped him free his own shirt from his waistband. The popping sound of the opening of the press-stud on her jeans exploded into the thick, heavy silence of the unit and Kris tensed, her eyes shooting open and darting quickly to the antique clock on the mantelpiece.

'Todd,' she got out. 'Your mother. What if——?'

He gave a muffled groan and glanced at his wrist-watch. 'She'll be hours yet. I know what she's like when she gets together with her cronies. However, I do see your point. This isn't the most private or comfortable place for what I had in mind, but I don't want to move, to let you go. Now I have you safely in my arms,' he added thickly.

His eyes devoured her bared breasts, his fingers gently cupping their fullness, his thumbs deliberately circling her taut, aroused nipples.

Kris caught her breath, her head falling back as she arched towards him. His hard length was stretched alongside her, his warm skin setting fire to hers where he touched her.

Tears welled in her eyes. 'Oh, God,' she choked. 'Why do you...?' Her voice caught in her throat.

'Why do you make me feel as though my whole body were afire?' he suggested huskily. 'Same question. And the answers are the same. We were made for each other, Kris Quade. There's no need to debate that.'

His words rang in her head and she felt a wave of self-contemptuous guilt. That might be true. It was true, she acknowledged derisively. But how could she be letting this happen when less than an hour ago she'd made up her mind to be firm with him, explain her position...?

Position? Kris almost laughed. This was the position her traitorous body had hungered for ever since the last time they'd made love. Love? It was lust, the very small part of her that still clung to control reminded her, and she stiffened.

Todd's eyes swung to lock with hers, one dark brow rising in silent enquiry.

'Todd, I don't think... I can't... My God, I'm so sorry. This isn't right, not for me,' she got out disjointedly through lips that had trouble forming the words.

His lips slid over her breast to tantalise one taut nipple and she shuddered. 'I'd say it was quite right. Perfect, in fact.'

'I mean...I don't mean physically.' She swallowed convulsively. 'I can't deny that I...that you——'

'That we're two halves of one whole,' he finished and Kris ran a shaky hand across her eyes.

'Todd, please. Let me just try to explain. I need to before——'

He gave her a crooked smile. 'This is one hell of a time to start a meaningful discussion,' he said, his fingers tracing the curve of her breast.

Kris's hand covered his and he sighed.

'OK, Biggles. But have pity on me and keep it short. I'm not sure how long I can maintain my attention, what with all the other more pressing distractions.'

Kris flushed, her eyes going of their own volition to the hard length of him, and she bit her lip, forcing her gaze to meet the wry amusement in his. She fought for resolve.

'When I...' She stopped and drew a steadying breath. 'When I married Kel it was... I'd known him almost all my life. We were married and life went on. All so steady.' Kris shook her head slightly. 'What I'm trying to say is that my life was all set out. It was to go on just the same until Kel and I were old.'

Kris's fingers unconsciously played with his. 'Then suddenly Kel was gone. And I missed his steadiness; I missed him so much I thought I'd die too. I never want to have to go through that pain again.'

'I can't bring Kel back, Kris,' he said, his voice low and tight. 'Lord knows that's the last thing on my mind right now. I'm selfish enough to want you too much myself. So much that I can't imagine my life without you,' he finished flatly.

'I want you, too,' Kris admitted, her throat thick. 'But I want more than... I need more than that, Todd. More than you're prepared to give, anyway.'

Yet for one electrifying moment she wished she could throw discretion to the four winds, wished she was capable of taking what he was so obviously offering.

But then reality took over and she dashed the wayward thought away in self-derision. She wouldn't be able to sell herself short and Todd Jerome wouldn't be prepared to pay the price she'd ask. Would he?

'And just what do you think I'm offering, Biggles?' he asked wryly. 'Come on, don't stop now,' he prompted softly.

'Well, an affair. Until you tire of me and...' She shrugged. 'Until you tire of me and don't want me any more,' she finished quickly.

'I'm sure by the time I'm eighty or so I'm going to be more than tired,' he put in wryly. 'In fact I'll probably be flat out exhausted after fifty years with you, Mrs Jerome.'

Kris turned to him in surprise and he gave a soft, rueful laugh.

'Not speechless at last, are you, Biggles?' His fingertip traced the outline of her mouth. 'I did have a plan of sorts. For tonight. There never was any client. When I arrived home I was going to suggest we go out for some supper, somewhere where they go in for soft music, romantic candlelight and...' He paused and sat up, reaching into the pocket of his jeans. 'And at the right moment I was going to snap this open and dazzle you.'

The dark velvet lid popped up, displaying a diamond ring that sparkled in the lamplight.

'Not quite the scene I set, but infinitely more to my taste.' He grinned and then the smile left his face. 'Will you do me the honour of marrying me, Kris?'

CHAPTER NINE

KRIS woke slowly, drifting deliciously out of sleep, and she stretched languidly. She sighed and opened her eyes to the unfamiliarity of a high-ceilinged bedroom.

Coming fully awake, she sat up, raising her arms above her head to stretch luxuriously. She had spent the night at Todd's family home and slept in his old single bed, because today was her wedding day.

She unfolded the fingers of her left hand and gazed down at the sparkling diamond ring that winked back at her.

A faint smile lifted the corners of her mouth as she recalled how Todd had slipped the ring on to her finger. And then kissed her hand, her arm, her shoulder, her throat, and, when she thought she'd burst with the waiting, her lips.

Kris flushed with the memories of her feverish response to him. Four weeks later and it hadn't cooled by one degree. The sensations had lifted her higher and then some, and she shivered just thinking about her reaction to simply a glance from his burning grey eyes.

She smiled broadly. She was in love with Todd Jerome and he loved her. Today they were going to be married and she felt wonderful.

Kris stretched again and lay back against the pillows. She could almost feel the touch of his hands, his lips on her body, and she laughed softly, a little disconcertedly. Tonight...

Her erotic thoughts were interrupted by a light tap on the door of her room and her heart raced as she reigned in her erotic thoughts.

'Kris?' Todd's mother opened the door and peeped inside. 'Are you awake, dear?'

'Yes. Yes, of course.' Kris pushed herself into a sitting position again.

'I thought you might like a cup of tea before we get busy.' She smiled. Her eyes were the same grey as her son's and she was short and pleasantly plump. 'I wanted to let you sleep as long as I could, but what with everything you need to do, the hairdresser, the...' She stopped and handed Kris her cup. 'Oh, dear. I must stop or you'll end up as flustered as I am.'

Kris laughed. 'I know I will be anyway.'

'Oh, Kris, I'm so happy for you and Todd.' She leant across and kissed Kris's cheek.

'Thank you,' Kris said sincerely.

'I know how much you love my son. And how much he loves you. I could see it from the moment I met you, the way you two were together.' She patted Kris's hand. 'Oh, my dear, if you only knew how worried I've been about Todd. I've been living in terror of his marrying some empty-headed little "yes" girl, and that would never do for him. She'd bore him to death in no time at all.' She smiled Todd's smile. 'I know he's met his match in you, just as his father did with me.'

When Todd's mother left Kris climbed from the bed and walked into the en suite. Standing in the shower, she let the water play over her body. She felt so alive. She'd never felt quite this way before.

Even with Kel. Kris allowed the thought to firm in her mind. But Kel was gone and her life had moved on, to Todd Jerome. And she'd fallen for him with every fibre of her being.

Switching off the shower, Kris clutched the fluffy bath sheet about her and shivered as she began to towel herself dry. Just the thought of him and every nerve-ending in her body tensed, as though waiting for his touch.

She felt a sudden urge to pinch herself, to prove she wasn't dreaming, that today she really was going to marry the devastating Todd Jerome. Everything had happened so quickly.

Kris walked back into the bedroom and sank on to the bed, lifting the pillow into her arms, hugging it to her, letting her thoughts carry her back to that wonderful evening, just four short weeks ago.

'Would it be so bad, Kris?' His deep voice had broken into her disbelief as she'd blinked at the glittering diamond ring. 'Marrying me?' he'd clarified.

'Todd, this is ridiculous. You can't be serious,' she got out breathlessly. 'We've known each other less than a week. We met under far from conventional circumstances. There's no way we should be making any momentous decisions right now. And——' Kris shook her head again '—we ... well, we have nothing in common.'

'I'd say we had something pretty rare in common,' he said softly, and Kris's traitorous body responded with sharp, painful ease. 'We could run a city on the electricity we generate.'

Kris flushed. 'That's not everything in a relationship. I mean, we have to consider that we come from totally different worlds. And I'm not sure I could cope with the kind of public lifestyle you seem to have. Quite frankly, I can't see myself as the wife of a future Prime Minister.'

Todd gave a soft laugh. 'My thanks for the heartfelt compliment, Kris, but I'm afraid that's all paper-talk. I don't have any immediate plans to go into politics.' His eyes momentarily left hers. 'I have enough work with keeping up with my business interests just now.'

'But Donna said——'

'What she'd obviously read in the newspapers and gossip columns,' he finished. 'It all began with a rumour and went on from there. I'm not denying I've been approached to become more involved in the political scene, but, believe me, Kris, I've never had aspirations in that direction.'

Kris held up her hand when he would have drawn her back into his arms. 'But that's what I'm talking about, Todd. Don't you see? We're like chalk and cheese—you must see that. You're city, I'm country.'

'What have you got against living in the city?' he asked rationally.

'Everything moves so quickly here,' she began, knowing her voice held little conviction. It was so hard to be clear-headed when her entire body cried out for him physically.

'You only need to move as fast as you want to, and besides, you do get used to it. And don't say you can't leave Amaroo,' he added when she would have spoken. 'I don't think your uncle would stand in your way if you wanted to make a life of your own away from the station.'

'I know,' Kris conceded. She had no ties on Amaroo, save the great emotional debt she owed her uncle and cousin for their support in the dark months after Kel was killed. But could she adjust her own lifestyle to his?

'So. I see no problem that can't be overcome if we work it out together.' Todd sighed, his breath fanning her neck, her sensitive earlobe. 'Oh, Kris. All I know is I've been searching for you all my life. And I want to share the rest of my life with you.'

Kris's eyes met his, took in the ruggedly handsome features, the firm line of his jaw, the sensual curve of his lips. Her body burned where it touched his, every nerve-ending clamouring for the release of the moment, and let tomorrow take care of itself. They lay together, his gaze holding hers, and Kris's heightened awareness of the hard masculine body beside hers surged through her.

Noise pounded in her ears, giving her a sense of vertigo, as her eyes stayed locked on his. Her breath caught somewhere in her throat as she tried to swallow. Then her heartbeats began an erratic tattoo at the unmistakable fire that flared in his grey gaze.

'Todd...' she breathed huskily, and she barely registered the glow of triumph in his quick smile.

'I need an answer, Kris.' His own voice was as unsteady as her own. 'Only "yes" will do.'

'Yes,' Kris whispered, the end of the word disappearing into his mouth as his lips claimed hers.

Sitting on the bed now, Kris's body remembered and stirred anew at those unbearably sensuous memories. And the month had flown by so quickly that she felt her feet hadn't touched the ground once.

Kris flew back to Amaroo to pack up her things, deciding what to keep and what to discard, while Todd had his time taken up organising his business.

Donna was ecstatic and fell into the spirit of helping to arrange the wedding, her smug smile reminding Kris just who had been the matchmaker in what she kept referring to as 'Kris's whirlwind romance'.

Both Kris and Todd had wanted a small private wedding, but, much to Kris's consternation, by the time Donna and Todd's mother had finished there were to be over a hundred guests.

Chairs, tables, a marquee, a band and a dance floor had been organised for the large back garden of the Jerome family home, which was built in a distinctive, high-set old Queenslander style with wide verandas on all sides, covered by a steep corrugated iron roof. It nestled in a quiet suburban street amid huge old trees, jacarandas and poincianas mingling with mango and silky oak, and Kris could imagine the green, well-kept lawns alive with the high voices of children filling the warm tropical air.

'This is the wedding of the year.' Donna brushed aside Kris's protestations. 'I mean, Todd's so well known, and you know how the media loves to go on about our family. We've had Amaroo for generations. We're the backbone of the cattle industry and all that.'

'The Sorrels might be,' Kris conceded. 'But I'm just an offshoot.'

'We're first cousins, for heaven's sake,' Donna exclaimed. 'You know, I've always thought we were Queensland's answer to Dallas's Ewings.'

'We're what?' Kris burst out laughing.

'We are part of the history of the cattle industry,' Donna remarked indignantly. 'And you're part of the Sorrel dynasty, Kris.'

Kris chuckled. 'Any minute now you're going to lapse into *Days of Our Lives* or *Sons and Daughters*.'

Donna pouted and changed the subject. 'And I can't understand why you can't have your honeymoon now. I mean, whoever heard of a miserly three-day honeymoon, even if it is in the romantic tropical north of the state.'

'Todd has business commitments just now, Donna, especially important ones that he can't reschedule. We're lucky to get the three days we're having.'

'I'm sorry, Kris.' Donna sighed contritely. 'I didn't mean to nag. But all I really want is for you and Todd to be happy.'

Kris nodded and hugged her cousin. 'I know. And we'll be going somewhere special after Christmas.'

Only later did Kris realise Donna had successfully distracted her from her intention to curb Donna's lavish wedding preparations.

*　　*　　*

And now the day had arrived. Kris stood in front of the old-fashioned mirror in her prospective mother-in-law's bedroom while Donna fussily rearranged Kris's hair and patted the skirt of the cream linen suit Kris had chosen for her wedding.

'You look divine, Kris,' Donna said and pressed her cheek to her cousin's, careful not to smudge her lipstick on Kris's make-up. 'Todd's a lucky man.'

'You've changed your tune.' Kris smiled a little shakily. 'I thought I was the lucky one because Todd was the catch of the century.'

'You're both lucky.' Donna chuckled. 'It's going to be the best wedding. Everything's gone marvellously and the sun's shining with nary a cloud in the sky.'

'Keep your fingers crossed,' Kris cautioned as her uncle tapped on the door to signal all was ready.

Kris's step faltered as she took her place on the carpet, which had been rolled out to make an aisle, ending beneath the colourful canopy of a huge poinciana tree. Its fern-like leaves filtered the harsh sunlight while its riot of vibrant orange flowers added vivid colour to the scene.

Taking a steadying breath, Kris found her eyes seeking the figure at the end of the aisle. Todd stood with his best man, the brother nearest his age, but her gaze was only for Todd.

Her eyes were locked on the back of his dark head, took in the broadness of his shoulders, moulded by the dark brown suit he wore. She knew the angle of his head, the way his dark hair curled over the collar of his cream dress shirt. He was so familiar. Yet suddenly so remote.

And she was promising herself to him for the rest of her life. A shiver clambered up the length of her spine as the band struck up the bridal march.

The time had come. And she couldn't move.

Todd turned then and his grey eyes met, held hers, the message in them burning deep inside her until it filled

her, drowning the sound of the music in her ears.
Warmth washed her face and her lips parted in a tremor
of a smile.

She unconsciously moved forward until she stood
beside him, in front of the celebrant. The slight breeze
lifted her fair hair back from her shoulders as she shot
a quick glance up at him. He smiled and her breath
caught somewhere in her chest.

The simple ceremony began. To Kris it took forever
and yet no time at all. She signed her name, part of her
amazed that the pen in her hand barely shook while her
heartbeats hammered erratically in her breast.

'Congratulations, Mr and Mrs Jerome.' Todd's mother
kissed them both and showered them with confetti.

Kris laughed breathlessly and Todd's arm slid around
her. 'Hello, Mrs Jerome,' he said huskily, that same
scorching intensity in his eyes as he bent to brush her
lips with his.

Kris's knees threatened to buckle beneath her as she
and Todd moved through the throng of wedding guests
to take their seats at the long tables assembled under the
marquee.

The catered meal was delicious, so everyone said later,
but Kris couldn't seem to taste the food placed in front
of her. Although the speeches were kept to a minimum,
as she sipped her champagne she began to feel just a
little light-headed and made a concerted effort to eat.

It seemed so unreal. Yet she could vividly recall her
heightened awareness of Todd's shoulder touching hers,
of the faint rasp of the material of his suit on the linen
of her jacket as his arm brushed hers.

They toasted each other with champagne glasses entwined and cut their three-tiered wedding cake.

Then the master of ceremonies was inviting Todd to
claim his wife for the bridal waltz and Todd led Kris on

to the portable wooden dance-floor that had been assembled for the occasion.

Kris felt herself melt into his arms; their bodies melded, flesh to flesh, bone to bone. Her breasts tingled where they touched his hard chest; her legs weakened as they moved together, thigh to thigh.

Todd brought her hand to his lips, slowly and seductively kissing each finger until his tongue-tip lingeringly caressed the palm of her hand.

Kris floated around the dance-floor on a wave of pure sensation. How she wished the day was over, that they were in their room at the luxurious resort in Port Douglas. Alone.

She slid a glance up at Todd to find his gaze on her, his eyes alight with the very same heat of arousal that she knew was reflected in her own. His lips touched the tip of her nose, her cheekbone, her extra-sensitive earlobe.

'Don't look at me like that, Mrs Jerome,' he whispered huskily, his breath against her ear fanning the flame of desire that radiated from the pit of her stomach. 'Or my reaction might shock everyone here.'

'Oh.' Kris's own voice was just as unsteady. 'What might you do, Mr Jerome? Or shall I call your bluff?'

'Not unless you want to be swung up into my arms and carried off to the nearest bedroom,' he replied outrageously, and Kris laughed softly, the sound causing him to tighten his arms about her.

'Then I'd best avert my eyes, hadn't I? In the interests of propriety.'

'And perhaps it might be a good idea for me to save my strength, hmm?' he teased, and Kris felt her cheeks colour.

At that inopportune moment Kris's uncle tapped Todd on the shoulder to claim a dance with his niece. Kris

couldn't suppress a chuckle as Todd groaned softly as
he reluctantly surrendered her.

The afternoon wore on and each time Kris's eyes met
those of her new husband her heartbeats fluttered in her
breast like a trapped bird. Then eventually it was time
for Kris to change into her travelling outfit.

She had barely had time to undress and fall into bed
the night before, but now she gazed around the bedroom.
Todd's sanctuary. It was small by modern standards, but
the light cream-coloured tongue-and groove pine walls
gave it a feeling of space. The ceiling, as in the rest of
the house, was high, and moulded cornices decorated
the corners.

A single bed, wardrobe, desk and large bookcase filled
the room, and there was an olive-green-shaded sheepskin
rug on the polished wooden floor.

Kris glanced at the books, running her finger over the
spines as she read the titles. Thrillers. Espionage. Some
heavy textbooks. And on the lower shelf some juvenile
classics. She pulled one from the shelf and found herself
smiling.

The Air Adventures of Biggles. So this was the origin
of his teasing nickname. Replacing the book, she turned
to her case.

The flight up to Cairns in north Queensland would
take them over two hours and then they would have
almost an hour's drive northwards along the coast to
their destination, the Sheraton Mirage in Port Douglas.
For travelling comfort Kris had chosen a pair of light
cotton trousers and a pale mauve-coloured tailored shirt.

Slipping out of her cream suit, she found a hanger
and crossed to the wardrobe, hanging the outfit on one
of the knobs. She donned the trousers and shirt and ran
a brush through her hair, stopping to gaze at the face
reflected in the mirror.

Kristle Jerome. Did she look different from the Kris Quade of a few short hours ago? Her green eyes were bright and her full lips curved into a quick smile.

You look positively smug, Kris Quade Jerome, she told herself and pulled a face.

Turning away, she pulled out the one chair in the room, in front of Todd's desk, to slip on her shoes. But she'd sat on something. A book. Kris pulled it from beneath her and went to place it on the desktop.

A newspaper clipping slipped partially from between the pages, and as she went to shake it back inside the book fell open and her attention was caught by a small photograph of her husband in cricket whites. Curiosity claimed her and she flipped to the front of what was obviously a scrap-book.

A smiling Todd at about ten years old gazed from beneath the caption 'Jerome Kicks Winning Goal'. Kris turned the pages. Either Todd or his mother had kept every clipping. Football games. School sports. School newspaper by-lines. And, towards the back, news reports speculating on his prospective political career.

There was one of the clippings Donna had eagerly pressed on Kris at Amaroo to show Kris just how handsome Todd was. And he was attractive, Kris acknowledged as she ran her finger softly over Todd's smiling face.

She turned the pages and there were the attention-grabbing headlines. 'Businessman Missing In North'. And 'Search Widens For Missing Pair'. Kris shook her head. It had been quite an adventure.

A couple of loose clippings slipped out of the back of the book again and Kris unfolded one and spread it out on the desktop. She gazed at the headline she'd uncovered.

'Business Tycoon Seeks Wife To Win Seat?' Kris frowned slightly, her eyes skimming the article. It seemed

the newspaper had run a poll and found the majority of
electors preferred a married candidate, as the retiring
sitting member was, to a bachelor. The reporter went on
to suggest an unnamed party official had leaked the fact
that there was more than a little concern about the
marital status of the rumoured replacement for the retiring member.

When questioned, the article continued, Mr Todd
Jerome had replied with the ubiquitous 'No comment!'

Did Todd set any store by this type of write-up? Surely
not. It was simply speculative and...

Her fingers stilled as she looked at the other loose
clipping. Half of the page was covered by a grainy print
of herself being lifted in Todd's arms at the air terminal
in Townsville.

But it wasn't that shot that held her attention. Just
below it was an even grainier print of two people locked
in an embrace that would have done an explicit movie
poster proud. It would have been difficult to identify the
couple involved had it not been for the setting, the
makeshift bed, the scrubby trees, the rocky ground, and
the crashed Cessna poised grotesquely on its back.

Two small full-faced photos of Todd and Kris were
inset in the larger shot and the headlines blazed. 'Two
Hearts Collide'. Kris cringed. How could any self-
respecting reporter...? Yet she was drawn to read on.

When the small Cessna fell from the sky somewhere north-west of Townsville last week it was more
than the impact of the crash that made the earth move
for high-profile Brisbane businessman Todd Jerome
and pilot Kristle Quade of Amaroo Station—see
photos above.

We've all heard of trains crashing as lips meet, but
is this all it seems? And was it really love at first sight?
Our reporter went straight to the horse's mouth and

asked Todd Jerome last night. Mr Jerome yet again made the very typical 'No comment'.

However, if ever a man looked pleased with himself it was the young financial whiz-kid. Rumour has it that Todd Jerome, founder of his own highly successful financial advisory firm, Jerome Enterprises, will be running with the opposition for the seat of Indooroopilly upon the retirement next month of the sitting member, George Beck, much renowned as a stable family man.

Mr Jerome was also making no comment about his political ambitions, but it can't have failed to occur to his party executive that a happily married man would be expected to poll far better in that electorate than a bachelor, be he ever so rich and handsome, as Todd Jerome undoubtedly is.

After all the publicity surrounding the crash, a wedding at this stage would certainly do no harm to his political career, especially when the prospective bride is the niece of well known grazier Ted Sorrel of Amaroo.

The Sorrel family is one of the few remaining 'old families' of Queensland's cattle industry.

Kris didn't need to read the potted biography that followed. She knew all about her great-great-grandfather and the history of Amaroo cattle station. Until now she had taken her background for granted. The sum she would inherit from her grandmother's estate in four years would hardly place her in the marry-her-for-her-money class.

And by all accounts Todd wouldn't need to marry for financial gain. He was extremely well off in his own right.

Kris glanced again at the newspaper articles. But would he make a marriage because he considered it to be pol-

itically advantageous? Surely not. Of course he wouldn't,
Kris admonished herself.

No! She shook her head. He wouldn't have married
her for... He loved her. As much as she loved him. Didn't
he? The end of the article leapt out at her from the pulpy
paper.

Love or not, the continuing publicity is sure to have
helped rather than hindered Todd Jerome's chances
in the upcoming political event. A less than cynical
onlooker couldn't have failed to realise the story of
'boy meets girl', in this case Todd Jerome and Kristle
Quade, 'and they live happily ever after', is straight
from the pages of the best romantic fiction novel. A
real vote winner.

A real vote winner. Kris's heart constricted painfully.
Was he using her in his ambitious climb to the top? She
was socially acceptable, certainly not poverty-stricken,
and although she was no beauty she knew she was
pleasantly attractive. And she'd fallen into his arms, a
plum ripe for the picking. The fact that they were physically attuned Todd no doubt considered to be quite a
bonus.

How could he?

Her whole body seemed to ache with the weight of
Todd's perfidy. She'd thought he loved her.

Kris stood up, the newspaper clippings crushed in her
hand. Deep inside she had known she was rushing into
this marriage. Why hadn't she trusted that instinct instead of allowing her purely physical attraction to
override her usual careful reticence?

Well, all his plans had come unstuck. Their sham of
a marriage, which had scarcely begun, was now over.

'Kris.' The softly spoken sound of her name made her
jump.

The door opened and her new husband stood framed in the doorway. He had changed his suit for casual grey denims and a pale grey and white striped short-sleeved sweat-shirt and in those few seconds, or hours, Kris drank him in.

His tall, hard body. Long, strong legs. Narrow waist. Wide, solid chest. Broad shoulders. Thick, dark hair. Her fingers remembered the rich, erotic feel of it.

And, lastly, his face. The attractive planes and angles of it. High forehead, the dark slashes of his eyebrows, the chiselled nose and square jaw. His compelling grey eyes, fringed by thick black lashes. And his mouth...

A wave of pure anguish coursed through her. Every ounce of her felt betrayed.

'Kris,' he repeated in that same sensual tone that her traitorous body reacted to with a will of its own, 'we should be leaving.'

Kris opened her mouth as pain and flagrant desire rose as one within her, but no words came.

Todd stepped into the room, took two steps towards her, a faint enquiry in his eyes, in the shifting of his brows. 'Kris? Are you ready to go?'

'No!' she got out, her voice hoarse and ragged.

He paused momentarily and then, as he continued forward, Kris was roused to action.

'No!' she repeated, her hand going out to ward him off. 'No! I'm not going.'

'Kris, what is it?' Todd had stopped in front of her.

She moved away from the desk, put a little space between them in the now closing confines of the small room. 'I'm not going, Todd. I can't.'

'What's going on, Kris? What's happened?' In one stride he had followed her and she shrank back against the bed.

'I want a divorce.' The word seemed to echo ominously around the high ceiling. 'I want an annulment or a divorce or...' She swallowed quickly, trying to rein in the hysteria that threatened to rise up and burst from her. 'I want to end this marriage...this farce...'

CHAPTER TEN

FOR long seconds his eyes burned into hers as though trying to see deep into her soul. Then he moved, went to clasp her arms, and Kris flinched back. Todd stilled and the air around them, between them, grew heavy and ominous.

The corners of his mouth lifted wryly as he took one slow step back from her, and then another. Still holding her gaze with his own, he felt behind him for the door and pushed it closed with a restrained click.

'What's this all about, Kris?' he asked quietly as he leant back against the closed door, folding his arms across his broad chest.

'I told you. I want... I don't want to... to continue...' Kris swallowed. 'I don't want to be married to you,' she got out in a rush.

Silence filled the room again.

'A little late for that, isn't it, my dear?' he asked levelly, and Kris's stomach muscles twisted painfully.

He deserved an explanation, she knew, but her vocal cords seemed paralysed and her heartbeats thudded so loudly that they threatened to choke her.

'Sudden change of heart?' he suggested mildly, his tone contradicting the anger in the set of his jaw.

His eyes were mere slits, his whole demeanour giving the volatile impression of a man held mightily in control. 'I mean, it's not usual for a bride of——' he paused, moving one tanned arm to flick an exaggerated glance at his wristwatch, and then returned his cold, grey gaze to Kris '—a bride of little more than four hours to suddenly want to cry off. The shortest marriage on record, surely?' One dark brow rose challengingly.

'I just want it over,' Kris said flatly, knowing as she uttered the inane words that he deserved more in the way of an explanation than that.

He smiled, and a shiver streaked up Kris's spine. 'You just want it over?' he repeated without inflexion and settled his shoulders against the door, crossing one jeans-clad leg with apparent casualness over the other. 'And that's it? No explanations? No excuses? Not even something like, "Look, Todd, I've got cold feet," to soothe my wounded feelings? Because, believe me, Kris——' he pushed himself upright and dropped his hands to his hips '—I *am* upset. Could you even imagine I'd be otherwise? That I'd just accept something like, "I just want it over," on face value and say "OK, so be it"?'

Anger rekindled inside Kris, an anger that part of her acknowledged as unreasonable. But he was the wrongdoer, she told herself. Not herself. She'd gone into this marriage for all the right reasons, but Todd Jerome clearly hadn't.

'You lied to me.' The words broke from Kris as she straightened, her own eyes flashing angrily as she faced him. 'You lied! This was all a set-up, wasn't it? And who knows how far back it went? For all I know it was planned before you even accepted Donna's invitation to Amaroo. And I fell for it, didn't I? I was such a push-over that you barely had to work for it. You mustn't have been able to believe your luck. You set the trap and I strolled in like a lamb to the slaughter.'

'What the hell are you talking about?'

'I'm talking about this.' Kris held out the crumpled newspaper clippings she still clutched in her hand. 'These excerpts from the scrapbook of the so famous Todd Jerome.'

'I still don't know what you're talking about,' he repeated, his eyes going to the ball of newspaper she held, and Kris sensed rather than saw the sudden pause he wasn't quick enough to hide.

Kris deliberately smoothed out the clippings and held them up in front of him. '"Businessman Seeks Wife To Win Seat". Very informative. And how about——' she showed him the other one '—"Two Hearts Collide". How romantic,' Kris stated sarcastically. 'And take note of the photograph. It appears that we were so lost in each other's arms that we were unaware of the photographer hovering overhead. Such a pity the helicopter didn't turn up a little earlier, then we could have really provided him with an interesting shot, couldn't we? Although somewhat X-rated.'

Kris took a few quick breaths to steady herself. 'What? No denial, Mr Use-anything-and-anyone-to-get-to-the-top?'

Todd took the clippings from her, his eyes moving over the print, before he in turn crumpled the offending articles and tossed them to the floor. 'You don't believe that, Kris.'

'Don't I? I think I do.'

'I didn't marry you to further my political career and even I couldn't have rigged the plane crash,' he stated firmly.

'Perhaps you're underestimating yourself?' Kris gave a sharp laugh. 'My first thought was that it had been set up as a political stunt, but I admit a plane crash is pretty drastic, let alone chancy, and I suppose you'd be no use to the cause if I'd written us off as well as the plane. Nevertheless, can you deny a candidate would poll better in an election if he was married, as that article suggests?'

'Of course I don't deny that. It's common knowledge. But, as I told you before, it's not my intention to enter politics at the moment,' he said shortly. 'And I didn't come out to Amaroo with the express purpose of meeting you, as that other bit of rubbish implies. If you remember, your cousin arranged a business meeting. And if you were looking at all this reasonably you'd also remember that I thought you were a man.'

Kris's resolve threatened to falter. He had been looking for a male pilot. No, she chided herself. He was smoke-screening. 'Perhaps that may be so,' she conceded reluctantly, 'but the whole thing played right into your hands. And you certainly didn't waste any time taking advantage of it. And me,' she added self-derisively.

'Kris, all this is ridiculous.' He took a step towards her, but Kris held up her hand.

'Is it? I think not, Todd. But it's my own fault. I got myself into it and now I have to get myself out of it. Against my better judgement I let you rush me into this travesty of a marriage. But now I've come to my senses and——'

Todd covered the space between them in two angry strides, his hands grasping her arms, holding her fast. 'You know why I married you, Kris,' he said earnestly.

'Yes, I'm afraid I do, Todd. Now let me go!'

'Never,' he said coldly, his eyes burning into hers as his lips slowly descended towards hers.

However, before his mouth could claim hers the sound of a soft, discreet knock on the door seemed to explode into the room, stilling them both.

'Todd? Kris?' Mrs Jerome's voice called apologetically. 'The driver's ready to take you to the airport.'

Todd recovered first, drawing a quick breath, his hands still holding Kris. 'Give us a few minutes, Mum,' he said, and Kris heard the other woman laugh softly before she, she thought, considerately left them.

'We haven't the time to continue this discussion now,' Todd stated. 'We have a plane to catch.'

'I told you I'm not going,' Kris reiterated.

'The hell you're not!' His fingers bit into the soft flesh of her arm. 'You're going to walk out of here with me. We're going to get into that limo and we're catching the plane to Cairns. Just as we planned. Before we fly out I'm giving a small press conference, which I had to agree to give so that our marriage ceremony didn't become a media circus. You'll be right by my side through all of it, and you're going to look as if you're enjoying it. We'll sort everything out later. In private.'

'You can't force me to go with you, Todd,' Kris said evenly.

'I can, and, believe me, I will. Even if I have to toss you over my shoulder.'

Kris's mouth opened in disbelief. 'You wouldn't dare.'

His lips thinned in a parody of a smile. 'If you believe all the rubbish in that article then you'll believe I'm ruthless enough to do anything.'

Kris's eyes warred with his and she shook her head. 'You can't make me,' she repeated with less conviction than she would have liked.

'You'll do it, Kris,' he repeated quietly. 'Because I'm not having my mother upset by the field-day the papers would have with this. She has no part in it, but she'll be the one most hurt. Along with your own family.'

Kris's gaze flickered. She'd forgotten her uncle and Donna. They'd be devastated, as would Todd's mother.

'So we walk out of this room arm in arm, like any newly married couple. We smile and we make our farewells. We drive out to the airport and then we fly off into the sunset,' he finished bitterly.

They stood silently, Kris valiantly striving to hold her ground, all the while knowing she couldn't put the other people involved through the newspaper speculations on their débâcle of a marriage.

'We'll discuss the rest of this later, Kris. You have my word,' he said with ominous quietness and Kris grimaced.

'Your word? That's pretty rich, Todd, considering,' she said and sighed. 'All right. We'll mouth the right lines, but once we get off the stage it's over.'

It seemed to Kris that the rest of that day—her wedding day—passed by without her involvement. Or despite it. She knew she must have played her part in their goodbyes to their wedding guests for there was nary a whisper of constraint in the tearful kiss Mrs Jerome placed on Kris's cheek or the bone-crushing hug Donna subjected her to before she climbed into the limousine beside her new husband.

The two of them sat side by side in the opulent automobile, not touching. The space between them could have been a mile rather than mere centimetres. And neither of them spoke. Kris wondered what the driver thought as he occasionally eyed them in the rear-view mirror.

After a couple of turns they were crossing the Walter Taylor Bridge and the luxurious car purred through Indooroopilly and Taringa and along Coronation Drive as it skirted the wide Brisbane River. In what seemed like no time at all they were through the city and Fortitude Valley and had turned along the access road to the airport.

When they reached the terminus Todd left the driver to take care of their luggage and with a firm hand on Kris's arm he moved them purposefully towards what turned out to be a room set up for their interview. Kris almost had to run to keep up with his long strides and she pulled back, causing him to tighten his hold on her as he turned towards her.

'I don't care to have to trot beside you like a subservient wife across a public airport,' Kris bit out softly, and his eyes narrowed.

'Never in anyone's, let alone my wildest dreams could you be described as subservient,' he said with equal quietness, and he began walking again, this time matching his stride more closely to hers.

'And Kris,' he said, his lips barely moving, 'keep to the script in there, or I warn you you'll regret it. Simple subservience would seem like paradise.'

Kris stiffened. 'Don't threaten me, Todd. Let me warn you it's not good strategy.'

'I'm not playing games, Kris. I mean every word I say. Just let me do all the talking.'

'Like hell I will,' Kris muttered under her breath as they entered the room. But she suspected Todd heard her defiant words for his fingers tightened portentously as the cameras flashed.

However, once into the interview Kris was relieved to do as Todd had commanded and leave the talking to him. In fact, later she was hard-pressed to recall a word that had been said.

In the small room the dozen or so reporters—and Kris recognised a smiling Matt Kane in their midst—fired questions non-stop from every direction, making Kris's ears ring. How did people cope with this type of barrage on a day to day basis? She could only breathe a heartfelt sigh of relief when Todd indicated the end of what Kris could only describe as a distasteful spectacle.

'What about a kiss for the new bride?' It was Matt's teasing suggestion and, to Kris's horror, Todd replied.

'No trouble at all, Matt.' His lips claimed hers before she knew what he was about.

Todd stood up then, effectively finishing the interview. Cameras and lights were dismantled and Todd took Kris's arm, resolutely moving her towards the door.

'Congratulations.' Matt Kane placed himself between Todd and Kris and the door. 'You certainly don't let the grass grow under your feet, Todd.'

'Can you blame me?' Todd asked drily. 'We'll see you around, Matt. We have a plane to catch.'

'Always in a hurry.' Matt turned to Kris. 'He must be a fast worker to have snapped you up so quickly. Want to make a comment, Kris?'

'No, Matt. She doesn't.' Todd's fingers tightened where they held Kris's arm.

'And masterful.' Matt grinned. 'OK. I get the picture. Seeing as I didn't get an invite to the wedding, at least let me kiss the bride now.'

He stepped up to Kris and planted a noisy kiss on her cheek. 'The marriageable female population will want your head,' he whispered in her ear and Kris couldn't suppress a soft laugh.

And the sound gave her the impetus to revive her flagging courage enough to firmly remove her arm from Todd's grasp as they crossed to the waiting aircraft.

Yet the sensation of Todd's mouth on hers at the end of the interview lingered as they took their seats in the aeroplane. A kiss to keep up the façade. But she hadn't pushed him away. Hadn't wanted to. Because of the reporters, she assured herself with little conviction.

Not that that explosive moment seemed to have fazed Todd. During the two-and-a-quarter-hour flight to Cairns he appeared to sleep, sitting back relaxed in the wide first-class seat.

Had he felt her instinctive response? Kris wondered, stealing a sideways glance at his strong profile. Of course he would have. Her hands tightened on the arms of her seat. That sudden kiss had slipped under her guard and she'd responded subconsciously. On a physical level.

Physical. That was where his appeal lay. And although her traitorous body hadn't yet learned to spurn him it would have to be taught to do just that. Because she couldn't love someone for whom she had lost her respect.

When they reached Cairns their limousine was waiting and Todd lost no time organising their luggage so they could be off on the hour's drive north to Port Douglas and their destination.

Even in her disassociation from the whole situation part of Kris's subconscious recognised the beauty of the almost uninhabited coastal scenery. The many small beaches the road skirted, some sandy, some pebble-strewn. The vegetation flowing down to the sea. And the incredible variegated blue tones of the vast Pacific Ocean stretching eastwards.

The sun was about to set as the driver turned the car into the Sheraton Mirage Resort and pulled up at its imposing and opulent front entrance.

In no time at all they had been shown to their room, a magnificent suite overlooking the acres of turquoise pools that lapped the buildings. Their luggage had preceded them and now, for the first time in hours, they were alone.

And Kris's overriding emotion was extreme fatigue. It seemed as though her body had paced itself to their arrival at their destination and now her aching muscles simply wanted to fall into bed and claim the peaceful oblivion of sleep.

The room contained two large double beds and she sank down on the nearest, slipping off her shoes as she did so. Todd had crossed to the sliding doors and was gazing out over the panorama of pools, palm trees and the shimmering dark ocean splashed by the rosy hue of the setting sun.

'Do you want to go down to the restaurant or shall we eat here?' His voice brought her out of her sleepy reverie.

'We had a meal on the plane. I don't think I'm hungry. I'm just going to have a shower and go to bed.' Kris slowly stood up and, with a sigh, walked across to her suitcase.

'Without finishing our conversation?' Todd strode across the deep-pile carpet to stand behind her.

'I thought we had finished it,' Kris said tiredly. She pulled her toilet bag from her suitcase and turned to face him. 'Or I had.'

He stood with his hands thrust into the pockets of his trousers, his feet planted aggressively apart. 'Well, I certainly hadn't finished.'

'I'm too exhausted to carry this any further tonight,' Kris told him and made to walk around him, but his hand came out to prevent her.

'That's too bad. Because I'm not.'

'Please take your hands off me.' Kris defiantly met his grey gaze.

'For heaven's sake, Kris. This is supposed to be our honeymoon.'

'I told you how I felt about your deception,' Kris began.

'And I explained that the article was pure unadulterated rubbish. Forget it, and let's get on with our life together.'

'We have no life together. Now let me go.'

'Just like that.' He made no move to release her. 'Did you expect that I'd be happy to leave everything the way it was before we left my mother's house?'

'I don't want to go over it all again,' Kris retorted. 'You won't smooth talk me, so you may as well give up right now.'

'Give up?' he repeated between clenched teeth. 'Oh, no, my darling wife. I'll never do that.'

His grey eyes held hers, his intention in them speaking louder than any words would have, and Kris felt herself shiver.

If he thought she was going to indulge in…in…well, he was going to find he was wasting his time. She had no intention of heaping mistake upon mistake by repeating what were now, to her, simply sordid moments at the crash site. She'd make that as clear as crystal right away. She drew on her resolve.

'And surely *you* didn't expect, after what I'd discovered, that I'd be prepared to join you in the time-honoured custom of the joyous bridal bed?' Kris shrugged his hand from her arm. 'If you're looking for a night of passion then you'd better start searching elsewhere.'

Determinedly Kris went to continue on her way to the bathroom but his hand on her wrist restrained her once more.

'Funny thing. I don't want to search for passion anywhere else. Not when I've got it all right here.'

His eyes had narrowed to slits as he gazed down at her and Kris's heartbeats accelerated, although she was unsure of the cause. Fear of Todd? Or of herself?

Her chin went up defiantly. 'You haven't got *anything* right here.'

'No? Then why is your pulse racing?' he asked casually, lifting her arm for emphasis. 'Admit it, Kris. You're as turned on by me as I am by you.'

Kris wrenched her hand from his hold. 'My God! You take the most massive ego trips. You think a woman only has to look at you to fall for your so obvious charm. Heaven forbid that she says no! Any minute now I'll expect you to throw a tantrum because someone's stolen your favourite toy. Well, this toy isn't going to be played with.'

His smile held no amusement. 'Careful, Biggles. If we're talking about playing games, you should know that massive egos love to sink their teeth into a contest.'

'I don't believe this,' Kris spluttered. 'You are by far the most arrogant, most...' Kris shook her head and moved away from him, her back to him. 'I can't believe everyone's seen you as the playboy of the century, the country's most eligible bachelor. You've certainly pulled the wool over a lot of eyes.'

'And I'm getting heartily sick of defending myself against truth-bending newspaper reports,' he said with sudden steely constraint.

'All right.' Kris swung back to face him and continued as though he hadn't spoken. 'You demand we talk, then let's talk. We have an eligible bachelor who has women falling all over him every way he turns. He's ambitious. He wants to step into the political arena. But being a bachelor doesn't sit well with his family-oriented constituents. So our future Prime Minister needs a wife. Enter someone with good family connections. As luck would have it, at the right moment, with free publicity galore.'

Kris smiled self-derisively. 'So you turned on the famous Jerome seduction techniques and I fell into your arms. Another success. How boring for you. I'd say you need have no fear on your perfect score. Any jury in the land would decree I was guilty on all charges. The great Todd Jerome came, he saw, and he conquered.'

'Don't be absurd, Kris. You're simply trying to cloak the real issue.'

His rational words only fanned the flame of Kris's anger. She could feel her control slipping from her, but she was unable to do a thing to stop it.

'The real issue!' She laughed harshly. 'Yes, do let's discuss the real issue. OK, I slept with you. You rushed me into this fiasco of a marriage. And now I want out. End of story.'

'By hell it's not.' He stalked across to stop less than an arm's length from her. 'Not from where I stand. And if you'd be honest you'd see it too.'

'See what? That I've made a complete fool of myself? Oh, I see that very clearly. Starting with that one-night stand.'

'It wasn't like that, Kris. You don't even believe it so—— '

'Don't I? I think I do. Although heaven knows why I considered marriage as a punishment for my indiscretion. A public flogging would have done.'

'The temptation to do something like that just at this moment is at an all-time high, believe me,' he said through clenched teeth. 'Now, if you can cut the drama for a moment I'd like to have my say. And, for the record, I didn't see our lovemaking as a one-night stand.'

'Well, I'm sorry. I did,' Kris told him, her gaze locked with his.

His eyes narrowed and she sensed that he was holding his tensed muscles in check. They stood transfixed for long, immeasurable moments, like fighters who had called a truce, with each expecting the other to transgress. And all the while the air between them sparked with electricity.

It was anger, Kris told herself. Pure unadulterated animosity. No more, no less.

But she loved him. The words sprang into her mind without warning and she almost groaned. What a laugh. She'd warned herself before. It couldn't possibly be love. Love was a gentle emotion. Not this aggressive, acrimonious confrontation.

'You're wrong, Kris.' Todd was the first to break the heightened silence that had stretched between them.

'About everything. Just trust your instincts, instead of——'

Kris made an exclamation of exasperation.

'Instead of deluding yourself about your reactions to me,' Todd continued determinedly. 'Face it, Kris. Each time we touch, the fire burns out of control. And if you imagine I couldn't get you into that bed then you're mistaken again. And we both know I wouldn't have to force you.'

'Why, you conceited——' Kris began, although she recognised some of the intensity had inexplicably left her voice.

He raised his dark brows. 'Conceited, too? Well, why not? I'd foolishly forgotten you had me pegged as a "love-'em-and-leave-'em" playboy. However, it appears I must be the conventional type. Perhaps I think that once I've bedded a woman I feel responsible for her somehow. If that makes me outmoded then perhaps we may have to put my tedious behaviour down to that, hmm?'

His cold grey eyes held hers and, by the second, she was beginning to feel more like a moth being drawn to a flame. For some incomprehensible reason her anger had cooled as she tried to sort through the mixture of confused emotions conflicting within her, her brain sluggishly striving to compute the meaning of his caustic dialogue.

Kris's mind caught up with the conversation in a rush and she felt herself draw an enraged breath through her quivering nostrils. Outmoded? Responsible? He was simply playing with her again, wasn't he?

'I can only suppose you consider me old-fashioned enough to want you to feel responsible for me, now that you've—how shall we describe it delicately—put your brand on me?' Kris arched her eyebrows. 'Well, let me assure you that, fortunately for both of us, I'm most definitely not the faint-hearted female you so mistakenly think I am. So there's no need whatsoever for you to feel any responsibility for me. And I don't even begin to believe that's why you married me.'

'You know why I married you, Kris. Trust me. Give me time to prove it,' he said with soft supplication.

All Kris's senses screamed for her to do just that. Capitulate. And it would be such a sweet surrender...

She could lean forward, rest her weary body against the solid strength of his chest, feel his strong arms around her. But she knew she couldn't allow herself that luxury. The doubts would still be there in the morning.

She gave a slight negating shake of her head as his hands came out to grip her arms. Her gaze flew to his set face, saw the angry passion darken his grey eyes, and fear tingled up her backbone.

'No!' The word caught in her throat as he pulled her against him.

CHAPTER ELEVEN

KRIS and Todd flew home on Tuesday afternoon, two strangers sharing adjoining seats on an aircraft. Only these strangers made no effort to speak to each other. An onlooker would have been excused for not so much as suspecting that they were newly-weds.

Newly-weds. Kris's heartbeats faltered, raced, as the scene on her wedding night played back in her mind, beginning with Todd's brutal kiss. Yet even before she'd begun to fight him he'd thrust her from him, his breathing heavy and ragged, his eyes sliding from hers.

Then he'd run his hand tiredly over his eyes. 'OK, Kris. Have your way and sleep alone. For tonight. But you and I are married and we're going to stay married.' And he'd turned on his heel and left the unit, closing the door with a restrained click.

Kris had fallen into bed and, although she had suspected that she would lie awake, she had been so exhausted that she had fallen almost immediately into a deep sleep. At some time during the night Todd must have returned, for when Kris had awoken the matching queen-sized bed had been slept in.

They had endured the following days in the opulent surroundings, walking warily around each other. More often than not Todd had been on the telephone—to his office, Kris presumed. For much of the time Kris had sat by the pool or taken solitary walks on the beach. And at night she had retired before Todd returned from wherever he'd spent the few hours after they'd formally dined together.

When the time had come to return to Brisbane, Kris was more than relieved.

Todd's grey BMW was in the car park when their plane landed. One of his associates had flown to Sydney on an earlier flight and had left it for Todd to drive home. They only had to collect the keys from the attendant.

Kris waited by the car, watched his tall figure as he strode towards her. His dark hair, touched with copper by the setting sunlight, lifted lightly in the slight breeze, and as he drew closer she could pick out the strands of grey flashing back from his temples.

And Kris missed not one small aspect of him. Not the thick richness of his hair, the cool grey eyes, smokily dark in the fading light, nor the hard planes of his ruggedly handsome face, the firm jut of his chin, the full, sensuous lips.

She swallowed a sudden dryness in her throat as her eyes drank in more of him. The thin material of his light apricot short-sleeved shirt hugged the hard contours of his chest, the sleeves accentuating the bulge of muscles in his arms.

He moved easily, shoulders squared, and Kris's eyes slid lower. The loose cut of his grey designer jeans failed to disguise the obvious strength in the long length of his legs as he closed the distance between them. A small pain began in the region of Kris's heart and grew, until she had to draw her eyes away from him for fear that she'd break down and fall into his strong arms.

'Shall we go?' His deep voice jolted her out of her bitter self-derision as he held the front passenger door open for her.

Kris's eyes met his, his chilling expression in direct contrast to the warm late spring day. Despite herself Kris shivered as she made herself step forward to sink into the plush interior of the quietly impressive steel-grey car.

Only as Todd took his place beside her did Kris fully realise the extent of the part she was going to have to play. And for how long she was going to have to keep up the pretence. In front of his family, his friends, and the media, which was so much a part of his life.

She folded her shaking hands in her lap and just at that moment Todd moved, to suddenly loom over her, and she stiffened, instinctively flinching back from him, her heartbeats thundering skittishly.

'Don't forget your seatbelt,' he said flatly, holding out the strap.

Kris took it, her fingers fumbling against his, and she felt her flush deepen as she studiously focused on the offending seatbelt buckle, struggling to fit it into its clip.

He calmly took it from her and shot it home, the sound echoing in the confines of the car, slicing through the tension that seemed to Kris to be pressing ever heavily in on them.

They sat side by side in silence as Kris waited for him to start the car, set it in motion. She swallowed as her nervous tension threatened to choke her.

'Relax, Kris.' His words, though spoken in a low voice, made her jump, and she thought she heard him swear under his breath. 'For heaven's sake, even if there was room in the car I'm a little too old to be seeking that kind of avaricious thrill, don't you think?' he bit out sarcastically. 'And, at the risk of disappointing you, I much prefer the comfort of a bed. So you can take my word for it—I'm not going to jump on you right here in public, believe me.'

Kris turned startled eyes on him, finding his hooded gaze on her face. 'I didn't...' Kris swallowed painfully. 'I didn't think you were.'

'No. of course you didn't. And you haven't been watching me twenty-four hours a day expecting me to take my husband's rights.' His hands tightened on the wheel until his knuckles showed white. 'My most humble apologies for misconstruing your nervous agitation.'

The tension swelled again, filled the car until Kris thought it had to explode. And then Todd sighed, somewhat diffusing the strain between them. 'Look, Kris. This can be relatively easy or it can be difficult. I prefer the former, and, quite frankly, I've got a pretty tough week ahead of me at work so I suggest we cool it for the time being, shall we?'

'I thought you'd already taken it as read that I'd keep face for you until we can get a divorce,' Kris said flatly, gazing at the deep shadows on the steamy asphalt and the neatly parked cars, but not seeing any of it.

He made no comment for long moments. 'I don't recall agreeing to a divorce,' he said, his low tone edged in steel.

'I've made up my mind, Todd. But if you're worried I'll behave like an ill-mannered shrew, don't be.' Kris grimaced bitterly. 'I recognise your high-profile position and I'll try not to disgrace you by acting like a fishwife and shocking your prospective voters, although it will be an uphill battle.'

'Look, Kris, this isn't the best time for this discussion. There are things relating to my job that I can't...' He broke off and swore under his breath. 'We just seem to talk in circles and, believe me, I don't need this right now.'

'And I do?' Kris wiped a hand across her brow. 'I've had enough of this conversation. Let's leave it that you have nothing to fear from me at the moment, Todd. I'll be concentrating on being goodness and light and getting the next few weeks over and done with.'

Todd went to comment, but changed his mind and, reaching out, he switched on the ignition and the engine purred refinedly to life. With a flick of the indicator he pulled out of the car park.

In silence he headed inbound on the Gateway Arterial Road, and for Kris every moment of that drive was agony. She could sense each movement Todd made beside her. Every muscle in her body throbbed and her jaw began to ache until she had to consciously make an effort to try to relax it.

She could barely suppress a sigh of relief when they eventually turned into the underground garage beneath the units. And there, posed nonchalantly against his car, was Matt Kane.

'This is all I need,' Todd muttered between clenched teeth, and his hand clasped Kris's arm. 'I know I don't have to warn you not to confide in our inquisitive friend over there,' he said quietly.

'Afraid I'll break down and tell all?' Kris jeered and his fingers tightened painfully, but before he could comment Matt was opening the passenger-side door for Kris to alight. Slowly Todd released her and she climbed from the car.

'Welcome home.' Matt planted a kiss on her cheek. Smiling, he handed Kris a bottle of champagne, and she took it in slightly unsteady hands.

'Thank you. On both counts,' she got out and managed a smile of sorts.

'Beware the bearer of gifts,' Todd murmured as he walked around the car. 'To what do we owe the pleasure of your visit?' he added with barely concealed irritation.

Matt chuckled. 'Gracious, isn't he?' he appealed to Kris. 'The casual observer would think he wasn't pleased to see me.'

Kris made herself smile. If Matt only knew.

'What do you want, Matt?' Todd repeated resignedly, leaning back against the BMW, next to Kris, and her skin grew hot where his thigh brushed hers.

'Would I miss the chance of welcoming you back from your honeymoon?' His laughing eyes went from Kris to

Todd's sceptical face. 'Which I'm being a pretty good sport about, too, considering how devastated I am,' he added.

'Devastated?' Kris repeated weakly, shooting a quick glance at Todd.

'Because he saw you first,' he told her with a grin.

Kris laughed. 'I'm beginning to believe there are some grounds for the rumour that you're a flirt.'

'It's all malicious gossip.' Matt made an exaggeratedly hurt face. 'Which I'm sure Todd has fostered. And warned you off me, too, I'll bet.'

'Sorry to dampen your flare for the dramatic, Matt, but we've understandably had other things to talk about these last few days,' Todd said meaningfully, and Kris flushed at his implication.

Matt glanced at Kris and raised his eyebrows. 'That's a lovely shade of blush you're wearing.' He shook his head. 'Damn! It's always the same. Todd has all the luck. He always did get to them first,' he said without rancour.

'I don't think you'll be upset for long,' Kris told him, and he beamed.

'Thanks for the vote of confidence,' he said easily.

Kris laughed softly. 'Would you care to come up for some coffee?' she asked quickly. 'Or perhaps a drink?'

'Thought you'd never ask. I'd love a cup of coffee.'

Without looking at Todd, Kris started towards the lift, leaving the two men to follow her. They stepped into the lift that would take them up to the unit, and as the lift doors closed Kris slid a glance at her husband.

Her eyes moved over him and, regardless of Matt Kane's presence, the air around them became charged, alive with the same wild, erotic magnetism that had begun to pull her towards him. In those electrifying moments she knew a reckless longing to throw discretion to the four winds, to allow the heady yearnings of her body to take command.

And then some semblance of reality seeped in, and with an almost superhuman effort she wrenched her eyes from his. Shame now held her as she gazed sightlessly at the plush carpeted floor beneath her feet. What could she have been thinking? Todd Jerome might still attract her, but nothing could change the fact of his duplicity. He simply hadn't been prepared to pay the small price of honesty and integrity that she'd asked of him.

When they reached the unit Kris left the men in the living-room and beat a hasty retreat to the kitchen to make the coffee, but it was some time before she could regain her composure. Her body seemed to be a war zone where shameless desire and self-disgust battled for supremacy.

Like an automaton she moved about the kitchen. Subconsciously she was aware of the murmur of voices from the living-room, but only as she prepared to rejoin the men did some of their words reach her.

'I can't confirm or deny rumours, Matt. You know that,' Todd was saying. 'But you have my word that you'll be the first to know when I'm free to make a statement. Till then I'd appreciate no speculation spread all over the damn tabloids.'

'Fair enough,' Matt replied affably. 'But I could also use a nod about whether I'm heading in the right direction.'

'Impossible...' Todd stopped speaking as Kris walked into the room.

Free to make a statement? Kris looked at Todd, but his expression gave nothing away. Did Matt know about Kris's intention to seek a divorce? He couldn't know...

She passed Matt his coffee and he took a sip.

'This is just what I needed. I've been on the go all day.' He grinned at Kris. 'A good reporter never sleeps.'

Todd stood up and took the mug Kris handed him and motioned for her to sit beside him on the sofa.

Rather than make an issue of it, Kris acquiesced. After all, what could he do with Matt Kane sitting opposite them?

Todd's arm slid around her, his fingers settling on her waist as he pulled her against him, and Kris's heartbeats skittered in surprised agitation. She glanced sideways, her eyes meeting those of her definitely unamused husband, recognising the obvious warning in their dark grey depths. She tried to move away, but he held her fast.

Matt immediately enquired about the resort they had stayed at and the conversation then turned to tourism in the state. And Kris found herself enjoying Matt's light, uncomplicated discourse, even if Todd added little to it.

After half an hour or so Matt stood up to take his leave. He made a huge show of kissing Kris before Todd walked with him to the door. And she suddenly wished she could beg the other man to stay.

In silence Kris began to collect the coffee mugs, taking her time rinsing them and adding them to the dishwasher. But eventually she had to return to the living-room.

Todd stood looking out through the patio doors, his back to her.

'I'm going to bed,' she said evenly, and he turned to face her.

'Kris.' His deep voice made her steps falter when every instinct told her to run.

He sighed and ran one hand through his dark hair. 'We can't go on like this. We have to talk.'

Kris's heart constricted for a moment before she took control of herself again. They'd talked before. And where had that got them? Precisely nowhere. She was suddenly completely exhausted and she had no intention of rehashing it all again tonight. She was going to bed.

'I'm sorry, Todd, I'm more than a little tired,' she began and when he muttered something under his breath that she couldn't quite catch she unconsciously lifted her chin, her green eyes flashing.

'I'm tired, too,' he said exasperatedly, 'and in no mood for another slanging match so I suggest we try to sort this out as sensibly as possible. OK?'

Sensibly? Was he kidding? Why prolong the agony?

Kris felt the beginnings of a headache and she just wanted it all over and done with. 'Look, Todd. I'm sorry about your family, about how they're going to take our——' she paused slightly '—our divorce. And about your career, but...' She stopped as his grey eyes narrowed.

Again a heavy silence fell and Kris's nerve-endings quivered as her stomach tightened. He stood with his feet apart, silently watching her, and when he spoke Kris started at the sound of his voice.

'And I'll say it once again, Kris. There'll be no divorce.' He took a couple of long, measured strides towards her and Kris made herself hold her ground.

'You have no say in the matter,' Kris stated boldly.

'The hell I don't,' he ground out. 'We're staying married, Kris.'

'Oh. And how do you propose to manage that? Hold me here under lock and key? You'd never get away with it. Someone would notice.'

'Someone like Matt Kane, no doubt,' he said disdainfully.

'No doubt,' Kris agreed and the air between them thickened again. Kris had to clasp her fingers together lest he see the tremor in her hands as he watched her, his grey eyes black with anger.

'You seem to get on well with Matt,' he remarked tensely, and Kris blinked at his shift in the conversation.

'I enjoy talking to him. He's quite amusing.'

'Amusing?' Todd bit off a mocking laugh. 'I don't think that's how Matt sees himself.'

'That's how I see him.' Kris shrugged placatingly, forcing herself to stand quietly as he gazed broodingly down at her.

Then Kris almost moaned her relief as he moved a few paces from her, shoving his hands into the pockets of his trousers, drawing the material tautly across his thighs.

'He enjoys baiting me through you. But I guess you know that, hmm?'

'That's not my problem.' Kris's voice wavered as she drew her eyes upwards over his flat midriff, her face flushing at the discomfiture her wayward gaze caused her.

'But I suspect you get some jubilant——' he paused expressively '—pleasure, knowing he's getting under my skin.'

'You're being ridiculous.' Kris folded her arms across her chest.

'Am I?' He raised one mocking dark brow.

'Look, Todd, this has nothing to do with anything,' she began and his arrogant dark brow rose sceptically again. 'You're over-reacting,' she continued. 'Matt's a harmless flirt. He'd admit that himself. And as for getting under your skin——'

Todd's eyes narrowed to mere slits and his sharp, harsh laugh drowned out her words. 'Oh, he does that, believe me. But I suppose you're used to it,' he added softly.

'Used to it?' Kris stammered as her heart leapt in her chest.

He swung to face her. 'Men finding you attractive.'

His deep voice flowed over her and Kris felt trapped, unable to move or speak, held in the thrall of his so tantalising charisma.

'But my problem is, I'm not,' he continued, taking a step back towards her. 'I very selfishly want you all to myself.'

Kris was unable to say a word, her voice lost somewhere in the tightness of her throat. She could only gaze at him in disbelief.

'But you have to know that, too.' He grimaced derisively. 'Don't you, Kris?'

With no little effort Kris pulled herself into some semblance of control. 'No, I don't. And I really can't handle this conversation now. I'm going——'

'To bed?' he said with ominous softness and came closer, barely an arm's length away from her.

Kris's face grew hot and she went to walk past him. His fingers firmly grasped her arm. 'Take your hands off me!'

'Not until I offer some words of advice.'

'Advice?' Kris felt a surge of anger mingle with her heightened awareness as her eyes held his. 'Advice about what?' she challenged, valiantly fighting that now familiar involuntary arousal.

'Simply this. You're married to me. For better or worse. That means you don't mess around with other men, specifically Matt Kane.'

Kris laughed mirthlessly. 'You're overstepping the bounds, Todd. Matt isn't answerable to you. And personally, I really don't think he'd appreciate being told what he can and can't do. And neither do I.' She shrugged his hand from her arm.

'You're my wife. And as such you'll stay away from Matt Kane. Do I make myself clear?'

'Clear?' Kris threw her hands up in disbelief. 'You have to be joking if you think I intend getting involved with anyone. Apart from it being totally ridiculous and unjustified, I've been taken in by one man already and I don't intend to repeat the mistake. Now, if we're going to get so far off the point then I think we should put an end to this discussion tonight because, as entertaining as it appears to be for you, it seems pretty much a waste of time to me.'

'Discussing Matt Kane for your entertainment is the last thing I'm doing.' Todd faced her, his hands now on his hips.

'Good grief, you're acting like a . . . a . . .' Kris sought the right description. 'A jealous adolescent,' she finished and then wished she'd not chosen those words.

'Jealous, I'll grant. Adolescent remains to be seen,' he said coldly. 'But where women are concerned, standing in queues has never been quite my thing.'

'Queues?' Kris repeated, her eyes blazing.

'Queues.' He smiled without a trace of amusement. 'Especially when that woman is my wife.'

'I don't believe this.' Kris strode past him towards the bedroom, but his hand snaked out and clasped her arm again, effectively preventing her escape.

'Or am I missing my chance?' His deep voice stirred the hair at the back of her neck and she shivered, her anger replaced by that same, far more dangerous emotion. 'Should I make the most of the situation, Kris? Do a bit of queue-jumping while I have the opportunity?'

CHAPTER TWELVE

TODD'S hands were on her shoulders, turning her back to face him. And she went to demur, but somehow, as his hands touched her, her anger appeared to evaporate as though it had never been. But not so the other, far more potent emotion.

He needed so little pressure to guide her and it seemed that she moved in super-slow motion. She was acutely aware of Todd's strong hands on her shoulders, of each finger splayed out, burning her skin through the thin material of her shirt.

She felt the brush of his breath on her temple, caressing her earlobe, sending shafts of pure desire through her entire body as each nerve-ending vibrated its excitement.

His eyes gazed hotly into hers and Kris was convinced she was drowning. She drew a short, sharp breath that hurt her lungs, a so exquisite pain. Then his head came down, his lips finding hers, and she closed her eyes as a lightning bolt shot from her sensitised mouth downwards to blossom in the pit of her stomach.

Her knees threatened to give way beneath her and she sagged against him, her body burning where it touched his. His mouth was locked on hers, his tongue-tip seeking the warmth within.

And Kris met him with all the passion that only he could ignite, could kindle with such consummate ease. They stood locked together, swept into the vortex of an arousal that had been simply lying dormant, awaiting a tiny spark to set its tinder-dry embers flaming, glowing,

growing steadily since their lovemaking the morning of
their rescue.

Todd's hands moved over her back, firmly moulded
the swell of her hips, settled her impossibly closer to
him, leaving her in little doubt that he was as aroused
as she was.

She moved instinctively against him and he groaned
softly, his lips sliding along the line of her jaw to nuzzle
her sensitive ear, down over the curve of her neck, to
settle seductively on the throbbing pulse that ran riot at
the base of her throat. Then his mouth was claiming
hers once again.

Kris was totally tuned to every nuance of his hard
muscles, each tantalising touch of his lips, and she almost
melted at the deep, liquid sound of her name as he
breathed it into her mouth.

When his lips surrendered hers, his fingers slipped her
loose shirt off her shoulder, his teeth gently nibbling the
bared skin, and she shivered her delight.

'We were meant for each other, Kris.' His deep voice
broke in to her consciousness, shifting her focus slightly
from the sensations he was creating. 'We've both been
waiting for this moment. You can't deny that.'

Realisation exploded, and with it came all the sordid
details. Kris suddenly froze, pushing against Todd's
body, surprise gaining her space, and she took two shaky
steps away from him, her back now against the wall.

'No!' The word burst from her and she saw him flinch.

'For heaven's sake, Kris, you can't just turn us off
like a tap.' His eyes were almost black with his anger.
'In another couple of seconds we'd have been in that
bedroom making love.'

A part of Kris stood off, watching, horrified by her
actions. Yet she couldn't allow him to make a fool of
her again. 'Making love?' Her lips twisted contemptuously. 'I'd hardly call it that. And I don't...' She

swallowed painfully. 'I don't want you to touch me again.'

Somehow she made her rubbery legs carry her into the bedroom and she closed the door, sinking on to the bed to weep silent tears.

He made no move to follow her, although part of her so wished he would.

And the next morning she found herself sitting staring into space or suddenly having to wipe more tears from her damp cheeks. By one o'clock she realised she was hungry and remembered she hadn't even eaten breakfast.

Wearily she made some toast and a cup of tea and sat down to force herself to eat. The walls of the large unit and its silence began to crowd in on her and on an impulse she flicked on the television set.

She spent half an hour not hearing a talk show and as the local news break came on she stood up to switch off the set, but she paused in mid stride when Todd's handsome face flashed on the screen.

Her heart constricted as she reached to turn up the volume. Had he been hurt? Please, God. No! A profusion of searing emotions raced through her as she struggled to understand the announcer's words.

'... when well-known accountant, Todd Jerome, presented his surprise report to the Royal Commission into Corruption today. Mr Jerome has been working with the chairman in utmost secrecy and his diligence has more than paid off. We spoke to Mr Jerome as he left the courtroom a short time ago.'

A stern-faced Todd gazed into the camera, replying carefully to the questions put to him.

'Is it true that the recent rumours of your intention to enter State politics were released simply as a front to cover up your work with the Commission?'

Todd gave a quick smile. 'Not purposely. However, when certain suggestions were made we decided not to refute them.'

'Then you never had any intention of running for the seat of Indooroopilly?'

Todd shook his head. 'No. I'm afraid not.' He looked straight into the camera and Kris could only stare at the television set, her mind turning over his words with painful slowness.

'Can you tell us anything about the threatening phone calls to your office this morning when news of your involvement in the investigations broke?'

'I can't comment on that.' Todd moved off camera and the reporter's face now filled the screen.

'We here at Channel Four,' the reporter put in earnestly, 'have reliable information that there have been calls threatening the life of Todd Jerome should he appear for the prosecution and that the police are taking these calls seriously. We will have further reports in our bulletin at six.'

Kris stood frozen, her mind scarcely taking in the report. What did it all mean?

She couldn't think. Todd had never intended going into politics. He'd told her that, but she hadn't believed him. Had she misjudged him? She rubbed her forehead.

A tiny glow of hope began deep inside her, but she couldn't allow it to spread. If she was wrong... She had to speak to Todd. Phone him.

She glanced at her wristwatch and realised he would most probably be somewhere between the courthouse and his office.

But she was far too keyed up to sit waiting and agitatedly she crossed to the door. She'd go for a walk in the fresh air, try to clear her head. Maybe she could then make some sense of it all.

The bright sunlight danced off the water of the Brisbane River opposite the block of units and she strode across the park to the pathway along the river bank, heading away from the city skyscrapers on her left. She followed the path as it ran beneath the Captain Cook Bridge and crossed in front of the towering rock face that was lit so spectacularly at night.

Eventually she found a bench seat beneath a shady tree and she sank on to it, absently watching a motor launch race by, leaving its wash slapping on the rocks below her.

Kris had heard of the recent Royal Commission set up to investigate organised crime in the state. Her uncle had often talked about it over the past months. But that Todd was involved in those investigations Kris couldn't quite comprehend, for it shed a completely different light on the terrible newspaper articles she'd read just after their wedding.

'Business Tycoon seeks Wife to Win Seat'! If he hadn't been planning to follow a political career then why had he married her? Had she gravely misjudged him? The spark of hope flared again inside her. Had he married her for the same reason that she'd married him?

Kris groaned softly. And she'd ruined it. She'd allowed a muck-raking journalist who had twisted the truth to destroy their marriage and turn it into the disaster it had become.

The reason for Matt Kane's interest had to have been his instinct for a story. Todd's story. The statement he'd wanted had nothing to do with their wedding.

Would Todd ever be able to forgive her for doubting him? She'd have to try to explain... But would he be prepared to listen?

How long Kris sat there she couldn't have told, for she lost track of time, only stirring when she realised the breeze had turned much cooler as the sun sank a little lower in the sky. She shivered and rubbed her cold arms with her hands.

Standing up, she headed back the way she'd come, and only as she walked up from beneath the bridge did she notice the flashing lights of three police cars pulled up outside the riverside units.

Kris quickened her pace as another part of the television interview came back to her. The phone calls. Someone had threatened Todd.

By the time she reached the front entrance she was almost breathless, fumbling with the key to open the door. The lift seemed to take ages to reach their floor and as she stepped out into the hallway the door to their unit opened and Todd caught sight of her.

Kris clutched at the wall for support and in that one earth-shattering moment she thought she saw her own relief reflected on Todd's face, a face she knew was as pale as her own. Then he seemed to draw himself up and came towards her, to stop in front of her. Slowly he shook his head and then folded her into his arms.

He had shed his suit jacket and removed his tie and Kris could hear the thudding of his heart beneath her cheek. She closed her eyes, her own heart swelling within her chest.

After that everything seemed to happen at once. She was back in the living-room and Todd was talking to a group of policemen.

It seemed Todd had returned home with the police to set up a recorder on their home telephone and found her gone. Because her handbag was still on the sideboard they had suspected the phone caller had made good his threats and taken Kris to use as a lever to silence Todd's incriminating testimony. They had been about to instigate a search when Kris had returned.

'Can't say we weren't relieved to see you, Mrs Jerome,' one of the young constables said, and Kris's eyes met Todd's from across the room.

The expression in their grey depths caught her somewhere in the region of her heart and her senses soared. Perhaps, just perhaps...

'We'd better set this stuff up anyway, just in case the guy does call here. How many extensions are there?' One of the policeman began unpacking the case he carried with him and Todd turned away to assist him.

Kris decided to leave them to it, only wishing they would all finish what they had to do so that she could be alone with her husband.

She walked into the bedroom, and stood gazing unseeingly into the mirror. Could this all be a crazy, incredible dream? Her life had changed so radically in just a few short weeks.

That she'd wanted, that she was ready to have her life change, she'd realised even before she'd met Todd. But she hadn't wanted to admit it for it had made her feel just a little guilty, as though she was being disloyal to Kel's memory and all he had meant to her. Kel wouldn't have asked or wanted her to feel that way. But that guilt was the reason she had run back to Amaroo from Townsville.

Lost in her thoughts, Kris was still standing gazing into the mirror when a sound behind her had her turning hesitantly to face the man who stood framed in the doorway.

She felt a warm rush of colour wash her face and a quite different warmth swell within her at the sight of him. If only he knew just how much she loved him.

He stepped into the room and once again Kris felt that same tension arc between them. She smiled uncertainly and his gaze ran over her, firing her already racing heartbeats. Drawing a shallow breath, she took a tentative step towards her husband.

Todd's eyes had followed her movements and a flash of pain crossed his unsmiling face. 'I guess we've got to sort out the mess we seem to have made of these few weeks.' He paused and shook his head.

'Todd, I——'

He held up one strong hand. 'There are things I need to say to you, Kris. First and foremost, I want to apologise. For taking gross advantage of you. From the moment I met you. Starting from when we were stranded out there waiting to be rescued. And I did take advantage of you, didn't I? I forced the issue, used the situation, which God knows was volatile enough, to get what I wanted. I had no right to do that.'

A pain began deep inside Kris, and was growing with each second. Had she misconstrued that earth-stopping moment in the living-room such a short time ago?

'I knew we were both honed to fever pitch out there. The seriousness of our predicament alone saw to that. But I had to have you. I couldn't seem to help myself,' he said almost to himself before he took a deep breath, his eyes holding hers. 'I really wanted you, Kris. Badly enough to refuse to allow the dictates of my conscience any consideration.'

He'd *wanted* her! A cold pain wrapped itself about Kris's heart. 'You didn't force me, Todd,' she got out through lips stiff with fear-filled tension.

Todd made a negating movement with his head, causing a dark strand of hair to fall over his forehead. 'That's incidental, Kris. I knew you were aware of me physically. I felt it with every movement you made. And, my God, I was so attracted to you. More than...' He grimaced self-derisively.

'But I don't have to tell you that, do I? I wanted you so much and I was even angry with you because you were prepared to let me think you were still married. I just pushed all rational thought aside. And I took what I wanted.'

Kris lifted her chin. 'I think you're being a trifle hard on yourself, Todd. When we——' she paused imperceptibly '—made love out there we…I'd say it was a mutual thing.'

His eyes were narrowed now and she could see the erratic beating of the faint pulse in his clenched jaw. 'But I instigated it. And it was so good between us that I thought when we were rescued that I'd be able to simply snap my fingers and you'd come running.'

He bit off an epithet as Kris continued to watch him, her mind in a turmoil. 'I don't usually behave that way. I'm not proud of myself, Kris, but I'd never met a woman who so totally discomposed me the way you did.

'Where women were concerned I'd always called the shots. Until I met you. And, as much as I knew you weren't indifferent to me, you made it abundantly plain that you weren't going to let me get anywhere near you.'

He took a couple of steps away from her, leant on his hands on the window-sill, his back to her for a moment.

Kris's vocal cords seemed to be paralysed and she felt as though her whole world, a world she had so recently allowed herself to believe in, was beginning to crumble beneath her, piece by slow piece.

Todd turned back to her, his hands shoved into the pockets of his suit trousers, his expression shadowy with his face back-lit. 'You implied all along that I was a playboy extraordinaire.'

He gave a harsh laugh. 'Some playboy. After we were rescued my confidence that I had you right where I wanted you went out of the window. You said we had to get on with our lives and I was filled with a dreadful fear. All I could see was you walking away from me. There was no way I could let you do that.

'I was up to my eyes working on that damn case with the Commission but I was so afraid of losing you that I had to find some way to hold you until it was all over. So I rushed you into marriage. I took advantage of you again. Another mistake.'

He shook his head. 'You know, it's really quite ironic. I've never walked away from a challenge in my life. I've fought for what I wanted. But this time...' He took a deep breath. 'When it came to the most important part of my life I did everything wrong.'

Kris was as pale now as he was. Realisation dawned. Did he mean——?

'So if you still want your divorce, Kris, it's yours. But,' he added quietly, his eyes burningly bright, 'for all my ham-fisted mistakes, I did, I do love you. So very much.'

Kris stared at him, trying to right her rocking world. Her mind spun topsy-turvily. Todd loved her.

She swallowed and a tear spilled over and trickled down her cheek. 'I don't want a divorce, Todd. I'm the one who made the mistakes. By not trusting my instincts. By not trusting you. I love you, too,' she said simply, her voice catching on a sob.

He stood unblinking for long moments before he moved. In a few strides he had reached her, his arms sliding around her, crushing her to him. One hand went to her head, his fingers in her hair, holding her face against his shirt front. He murmured soothing, unintelligible words, his lips soft against her temple. Then he swept her into his arms, swinging her around, only then letting her feet slide to the floor.

'My God! What fools we've both been.'

Kris nodded and rested her hand tenderly along the line of his jaw. 'I was so attracted to you, from the moment we met. It scared me to death. So much so that I'm afraid I did try to use my marriage to defuse the situation.' Kris pulled a rueful face.

'I was so angry when I realised you felt you needed to do that.' Todd sighed. 'I found myself baiting you mercilessly about your fidelity. I was determined to prove you couldn't resist me.'

'Another success,' Kris said softly, letting her finger settle on his lips. 'But when I proceeded to fall into bed with you I was absolutely ashamed of my behaviour. It was so much more than...' Kris flushed, unable to finish. 'I mean, my marriage to Kel had been so happy but...' She shook her head. 'I was eaten up by guilt. Because you made me feel the way you did. I couldn't help feeling I was being unfaithful to Kel. It was totally unreasonable, I know, because Kel would have been the last person to...'

Kris sighed. 'You were right, Todd, when you implied I'd stopped living when Kel died. In a way I did. And I think I was just coming to terms with that when I met you.'

'Oh, darling.' Todd shook his head. 'I was so consumed by jealousy when I said that. And afterwards I couldn't believe I could have been so cruel. My God, you don't know how contemptible I felt. I didn't mean to hurt you.'

Kris brushed a tear from her cheek and Todd's arms tightened. She could hear the thunderous thudding of his heart.

'Don't cry, darling. Oh, Kris. I love you so much.'

She raised her head, looked up at him in wonder, and his hands moved to cup her face, his thumbs wiping the smudge of tears from her cheeks. 'Didn't I make that painfully obvious?' he asked huskily and she could only shake her head.

'Only to someone who was thinking rationally. Which I wasn't.' Kris smiled shakily. 'But I began to hope when I saw the news report on television. About your non-existent political career.'

'I was sworn to secrecy about that and I was just about to race home because I was free to explain it all to you when I received that blasted telephone threat. When I arrived to find you gone I thought you'd been kidnapped. God, I never want to go through that again. If I'd lost you...' He closed his eyes for long moments, pain tightening his jawline. Then he gazed down at her. 'I do love you, Kris. And I've never said that to any other woman.' His voice was huskily sincere.

'I love you, too, Todd. So much.'

But her words were lost as his lips claimed hers with a passion that startled and then inflamed her. They clung together, bodies moulded, and Kris met his fervour with her own. That instant seemed to be held transfixed. They alone existed, each for the other, for an immeasurable, so ardent moment in time.

When they broke breathlessly apart Todd sank down on the bed, pulling Kris on to his lap. He was breathing as though he had been running and with a soft laugh he rested his lips in the velvety hollow at the base of her throat.

'Mmm! You feel so good, Mrs Jerome,' he said thickly and raised his head to look into her eyes.

She put her finger gently on his lips. 'Can you forgive me for not trusting you? For believing that wretched newspaper report? My only defence is that Kel's death really set me back on my heels, made me suspect and evaluate everything. I think subconsciously I was afraid to let myself trust a situation where I was happy. I was half convinced the bubble would burst. And it was such common knowledge that you had your choice of any number of attractive women.'

Todd laughed. 'More paper-talk. But I did use my visit to Amaroo as a cover for some of my investigations in Townsville. I didn't know it would lead me to someone who would become my reason for living. No one has ever held a candle to you, my love.'

She put her lips against the roughness of Todd's cheek, and gently kissed one eyelid and then the other before pulling back to look at him.

'I'm not dreaming this, am I?' he asked huskily. Kris laughed softly. 'Not unless we both are. Oh, Todd. I love you.'

'The feeling's most decidedly mutual.' Todd ran his fingers down her bare arm, his grey eyes bright with un-disguised desire. 'From the moment you stepped out of those baggy overalls——' his fingertip traced the edge of her blouse to pause in the valley between her breasts '—I was yours.'

'I'd never have known it,' Kris teased lightly, her nerve-endings reacting deliciously to his touch. 'You made yourself as objectionable as possible. Women drivers, indeed!'

Todd chuckled softly. 'I can't believe I was so crass. However, in my defence, there were extenuating cir-cumstances, my love. The taxi I'd taken to the airport had had a close shave with a car and the other driver happened to be female. She was distracted by her kids in the back seat and very nearly wiped us and herself out so it was a case of shocks all round.

'Apart from that I'd just seen you without your dis-guise and I didn't know what had hit me. I felt as though you'd reached out and taken my heart in your hands. It was a completely new sensation and I totally blew my cool. When that gorgeous hair fell out from under your cap——' he picked up one fair strand, let its silky texture curl around his finger '—I wanted to make love to you right there and then.' His smile disappeared. 'I felt as if I'd been hit by a sledge-hammer. My God, Kris, I didn't know if I was on my head or my heels.'

Kris laughed a little embarrassedly. 'You did a fantastic job of hiding it. In fact, you deserved an Oscar for your performance.'

'My natural animal instinct for self-preservation must have taken over,' he said derisively. 'And I ended up acting like a prize fool. I'd never had a situation I couldn't control. Until then. The plane crash was almost an anticlimax.'

He chuckled at her disbelieving expression. 'Still, at least it meant I had you sort of relatively confined. I couldn't complain about that. But when I finally had you in my arms, everything intensified. I found I never wanted to let you go. I touched you and...' He shook his head dazedly. 'That's all it took, Kris. Just a touch. And I knew without a doubt that you were the one I'd been waiting for all my life.'

He drew a ragged breath. 'My self-assurance went out of the window. Especially when Matt Kane turned up like the proverbial bad penny and oozed charm. I could have torn him limb from limb.'

'I suspect he knew that,' Kris put in with a smile.

'Yes. Well, he sure pushed the right buttons. And out came the most ridiculous behaviour on my part. I couldn't believe I was ordering you to stay away from him.' He grimaced self-derisively. 'I discovered I wasn't as self-contained, as civilised as I'd thought I was.'

'You did beat your chest rather marvellously,' Kris teased.

A dull flush coloured the line of his cheekbones and Kris couldn't suppress a chuckle.

'I was a man possessed.' He feigned affront. 'I fully intended showing you just how much you wanted me. But when it came to the crunch I was afraid to risk alienating you completely. When you backed away from me after our wedding I all but fell apart. I'm amazed I kept my sanity.

'On our wedding night I was a desperate man who just made an absolute hash of everything he did and said. I wanted to make love to you so much, but not in anger. I was too afraid of losing you.' He shook his head. 'You see, I couldn't and still can't imagine my life without you.'

They looked into each other's eyes and the flame flared, engulfing them.

Todd shifted her on his lap. 'Do you suppose,' he said softly, 'that we can start our marriage all over again? From tonight?'

Kris flushed at the light in his grey eyes. 'Well, you could try bringing on some of the famous Jerome seduction techniques you've previously demonstrated so well.' The corners of Kris's mouth lifted in amusement at his grimace.

'Oh, yes,' he said ominously. 'What was my rating? Eleven out of ten, wasn't it? Have I created an unrealistic precedent?'

'Perhaps we'd better do a re-evaluation. That was hardly a true test,' Kris told him with mock seriousness. 'Rather like wind assistance on a record-breaking sprint. I mean, the situation, the romantic setting, not forgetting I was a real push-over and you knew it. It was too easy.'

'It was hardly that. And I was the one bowled over.' Todd laughed. 'But about this re-evaluation. It's hours until nightfall. I wouldn't like to have something like that hanging over my head for so long. Would you care to take pity on me and put me out of my mystery?'

Kris appeared to give his suggestion great thought. 'Only if your intentions are as honourable as you claim, Mr Jerome.'

'The most honourably dishonourable, Mrs Jerome,' he assured her, gently pushing her backwards on to the bed. 'Should we wait until tonight?' he asked half seriously. 'I mean, would you prefer that we reconstruct the scene so we can have some stars overhead, perhaps?'

Kris met his gaze. 'I was rather depending on you for the stars.'

'Ahh,' he murmured huskily. 'Is that another challenge, Biggles?'

'I don't think you need worry,' she said assuredly. 'Wind assistance or not, your track record is pretty remarkable.'

As they gazed at each other they both began to laugh. Then suddenly their laughter faded and they melted into each other's arms.

POSTCARDS FROM EUROPE
HARLEQUIN PRESENTS®

Hi—

I'm in trouble—I'm engaged to Stuart, but I suddenly wish my relationship with Jan Breydel wasn't strictly business. Perhaps it's simply the fairy-tale setting of Bruges. Belgium is such a romantic country!

Love, Geraldine

Travel across Europe in 1994 with Harlequin Presents. Collect a new Postcards From Europe title each month!

Don't miss
THE BRUGES ENGAGEMENT
by Madeleine Ker
Harlequin Presents #1650

Available in May, wherever Harlequin Presents books are sold.

HPPFE5

MILLION DOLLAR SWEEPSTAKES (III)